The Crown of Ash and Shadow

by

C. M. Hano

Hearts Of Dalaria

The Crown of Ash and Shadow

Cover Art by *Lea Schizas*

The Wild Rose Press, Inc.
PO Box 708
Adams Basin, NY 14410-0708
Visit us at www.thewildrosepress.com

Publishing History
First Edition, 2025
Trade Paperback ISBN 978-1-5092-6279-3
Digital ISBN 978-1-5092-6280-9

Hearts Of Dalaria
Published in the United States of America

Dedication

To anyone who has ever felt like they were not worthy
of love, you are.

Prologue

Screams of terror echo throughout the brisk night air. The mist is thick and even with my night vision; it is difficult to see. Tika, God of dragons, my father, disappeared just before the fog settled. We were heading back from the fight in Ziran. Mother sent word down their bond to my father that the skies were burning.

"Father," I cough as I try to speak. This is not a typical mist; it is smoke from a fire. Looking below me, I can see the orange glow and feel the heat rising from the lower level as I glide down. My home has turned into ash.

"Jaxx!" Mother screams my name as I land on the ground. My wings dragged behind me.

"What happened?" Black soot has covered her once flawless face. Her hair turned discolored and disheveled from the ash filling the air.

"They came out of nowhere." Her voice is hoarse. "Your brother, you must save him. The Dark Wizard wants him."

"Where is Father?" Her eyes shoot past me, and as I turn, I see a hooded figure fighting with my father. Shadows swirl all around them as more dragon fire rains down from above.

"Tika." I watch in terror as Mother runs to aid Father in his fight. Before I can catch her, a shadow dragon blocks my path. Unsheathing my swords, I charge at the beast.

"Traitor," I scream, and it laughs while using one talon to block my blades with an unbearable amount of force, knocking me into the stone wall of a burning building. With a loud crack, the back of my skull connects with the wall, and darkness consumes me.

Through fading vision, I see a dagger of bone pierce through Father, and flames of midnight engulf Mother.

The smell of ash fills my nose as my eyes flutter open and the painful memory of last night comes flooding back. Rising slowly to my feet, a wave of nausea hits me and my world spins for a small second. Dried blood stains the back of my head where it hit the wall. I feel no scar.

As my world stops spinning, I am confronted with the remains of Bavilon, my home. The once peaceful village, protected and ruled by a god, is now nothing but blood and ash. There are no houses to rebuild and no bodies to bury.

I don't care about anyone else. Running to the last spot I saw my parents, I only caught sight of their jeweled rings. A golden band with an embellished dragon with a ruby for an eye, worn by Mother. Given to her on the day Father married her.

Tears stream down my face as I clean my parents' rings off. Something on the inside of their bands catches my eye. The one worn by Mother reads: You are the shadow light that guides me through the darkest of times. The one worn by Father reads: You are the heartbeat to my very soul.

Falling to my knees, I struggle against the anger

and grief swallowing me. Fueling my soul to seek vengeance for not just my parents, but my home and the people of Bavilon.

The distant whines of a baby catch my attention. Tucking my parents' rings in my breeches pocket, getting to my feet, I run to where our house used to be. As I approach the pile of ash, the burning glow of light surrounds my baby brother. Leaning down, it fades with my touch.

Those two bright green eyes look at me as his cries are soothed with a thumb in his mouth.

"It is okay, Calian. I will keep you safe." Wrapped in a crimson wool blanket, unscathed by the assault on our lands, Calian is the second-born son of Tika and Carlaian. "To keep you safe, I will hide you in the realm of humans and keep my distance from you. Until that day comes, I will give you these."

Tucking our parents' rings inside his blanket, I ensure they are safe before taking flight across the sea, into the Kingdom known as Greveil. In the night's dark, I place him on the stone steps leading up to the palace. Conjuring up a parchment, I write a message to whoever should find him.

"Who are you?" a calm female voice asks from behind me. Turning, I can see the midnight-colored skin of a young woman.

"Please," my voice is unrecognizable with the croak that escapes. Without hesitation, the woman reaches out her arms and takes my sleeping baby brother from me. Handing her the note, I did not wait for another second before taking flight. Tears burn in my eyes at the thought of never seeing my baby brother again.

Part One: Before A Bond is Broken

Chapter One

Jaxx
227 Years Later

The scent of ale and seared meat has my stomach grumbling with hunger. My place on a corner table is solitude for me. No one comes near me. Everyone in this town knows who I am and what will happen if they cross me.

Tonight, I am in the mood for something a little more delectable than a hog. Scanning the room, I see some tavern ladies putting on their best show to win over the coin of any nobility. I spit at their feet. These lords and ladies that dishonor their vows by sleeping with someone other than their betrothed or life partner. They think they are better than everyone lower than them in status. Because they were born into generational wealth, they can break all the rules.

They have all become complacent. And I intend to take advantage of that any way I can.

I take another sip of my rum, letting the warmth fill my chest before someone takes the seat across from me. At first, we exchanged no words. When I make eye contact with the young woman, I notice she is hiding half of her face with a hood. "Are you him?"

"Depends on who 'him' is," I answered, leaning back against the brick wall.

"The Hooded Mercenary," she whispers.

"Nope. Never heard of him."

"Bullshit." She fumbles with her pocket and then unfolds a parchment with my exact picture drawn on it. "This is you."

I take it and examine the words beneath my nickname. Thief, murder, treason, and dishonoring a man of noble birth. A verbal laugh escapes me with the last crime. His daughter was of consenting age, and I did nothing but let her suck me dry. She was curious about what a cock tasted like before she got married. Who was I to deny the young woman in need?

"This isn't me, and if it were, I wouldn't be making deals in a public place full of watchful eyes and listening ears." I crumple the paper, my fingers itching to use my essence, but control is one of my many strengths. "Go away."

The paper smacked her in the face. "Please, I can pay you."

"I said—" My words died off as an exceptionally large coin purse thumped to the tabletop between us. I released a long sigh and leaned forward, whispering, "Meet me in the alley in fifteen minutes."

When she nodded, I drained the last of my drink and then quickly exited out the side door.

The brisk night air sent a shiver up my spine, my wings aching to be released. I checked my surroundings, ensuring no one could spot me, and dropped my glamour to stretch them out. It was the best feeling in the world, not having to hide them. Normally, I don't, but in a crowded room like that, they would smack into people left and right, and my wings are overly sensitive.

"Not sure you should do that right now." I turned to my right, and in the darkness of the back alley was a shadowed figure of a young woman. "I hear having dragon wings is exceedingly rare in Dalaria. And even more so in Greveil."

"I wish you hadn't seen me." I felt my green flames dancing along the palms of my hands, ready to be released.

"Why?" Her soft footfalls slowly approached me. I could see her clearly with my night vision. She had her long auburn hair braided to the waist of her pants. She had two shimmering daggers strapped to her outer thighs. Gods, she was beautiful. My cock raised its head, and I invisibly commanded it to stop. "Are you going to kill me now?"

The woman's dark blue eyes twinkled with mischief. She was a foot away from me, but her lilac scent was overtaking my senses. I brought my flaming fingers up to her face, skimming close enough to warm but not hurt. "That depends on you, wildcat."

"Wildcat? Is that your idea of a nickname? You don't know me well enough to name me something besides what my mother gave me," she said.

My eyes trail her from head to toe, slowing to soak in the curves of her hips and breasts that I can see myself marking. "And if I wanted to get to know you?"

Out of nowhere, I felt the stall pressing against my back. Without realizing it, I had just given up my advantage to this—

"You don't want to get to know me," she whispered, then in the blink of an eye, her daggers were in an 'X' shape at my throat. My cock instantly hardened. Then those deep blues of hers looked down at where her body pressed against mine, and I knew she felt how hard I was. A devious smile came across her face, and she looked at me, saying, "You have my attention. Got a room?"

Fuck yes.

"Top floor, private suit," I answered, sounding like a whipped mutt.

"Meet you there."

Then she was gone. The door swung closed, and I had to blink away the lust and momentary confusion from our encounter to focus. I went back inside when the door flew open, knocking me in the nose. I tasted blood a second later.

"My apologies." It was the woman from before.

"What do you want?" I snapped.

"I need you to kill someone for me."

"What did they do?"

"Why does it matter?" I could hear the confusion in her tone.

"Because…" I wiped the blood from my nose, cracking the bones back into place, then said, "I don't kill innocence."

"She is not. I have proof." The woman withdrew more papers from her pockets. I flipped them open one by one. Depicted drawings of a man and woman in many sex positions. "That woman fucked my husband on our wedding night."

"Really? Was this before or after the vows?"

She opened her mouth and then closed it again before stuttering. "It…well….I mean, it was the same day. Just kill her."

I tossed the paper back to her. "No."

"But what of this?" She revealed the other half of

her face. The scarred half of her face revealed her mouth and parts of her facial structure, and she was missing her right ear.

"How did she manage that?"

"There was a fire. I informed her I would report them, and after my husband and I had consummated the marriage, I woke up the next morning to find our house on fire."

"And you saw her fleeing the scene of the crime?" I asked.

Her silence confirmed this. Then she threw me one last drawing, exclaiming, "Here is what she looks like."

Taking money from a wealthy family could be useful for the next gathering. It would feed everyone for months. "Very well."

****

Abbygale

This is not where I was supposed to be tonight.

If my sister knew I was away from the castle tonight past curfew, she would have me thrown in the stockade as an example. Not really, but ever since she became queen of Orion Fortress, she has been behaving more like our mother than ever before. That is why I am out. Venturing into a tavern in a small town within Greveil. Once the barrier dropped, there was not much time for us to venture across the sea. But I made time. Kaleigh does not know about it.

If she knew what I was about to do with a stranger in this room, why, well, I cannot imagine it. I am a grown-ass woman, making my own decisions. It is part of life. The door creaked open. My daggers were in my hands, ready.

"Wow, I thought we were coming up here for fun,"

the man with the dragon wings said, holding his hands up in surrender. He used his glamour to conceal his wings again, and a slight seed of disappointment settled in me.

"I suspect fighting with you would be fun," I responded. I was not usually this flirtatious with the strangers I welcomed. But something about this man had my core coming to life.

He smirked before closing the distance between us in two quick strides, but stopped when the tip of my right dagger pressed against his throat. "Why did you ask to meet me up here? To fuck?" He narrowed his eyes, but I kept smiling. "No, you don't want to fuck or fight. You want to disobey. I can see the defiance dancing in those eyes. So, who is it? Your husband?" His eyes went to my right hand. "Nope, cannot be. Father? You must be of noble birth."

"You will never guess correctly. Now, take off your clothes and get on the bed," I commanded. His hand snapped to my throat and lifted me, forcing me to the wall, but my other dagger was at his throat before he could kill me. I knew he could with those powerful flames, but I did not care. My heart was thundering in my ears at this point.

He leaned forward and took a long inhale of my scent. Then his eyes came to life like two blazing emeralds for a small second. I was afraid. Not that he would end my life, but that he would find out that I was the princess of Orion. If he knew who I was, it would be over before I wanted it to be. "I wonder if you taste as good as you smell."

Okay, that is not what I was expecting him to say.

"Then why don't you have a taste?" I whispered.

He leaned forward to kiss me, but I turned my face away. "I have rules."

He hummed against my neck. "And those are?"

"No kissing. No fucking. Just oral and hands, got it?"

The dragon shifter stepped away, letting my feet hit the floor, then smiled. "Fine."

We both discarded our clothes on the floor with our backs to one another. I was not ashamed of my body, but the only man I had seen naked was Tristan. My eyes swelled with the sudden memory, but I swallowed it down. I counted down to three before turning, but before I could, two warm hands gripped my hips, and lips landed on my neck, causing me to flinch.

"Did I catch you off-guard?"

"You just surprised me. Now put your mouth to effective use before I change my mind."

"You're feisty, Wildcat."

"And you've got to stop calling me that."

His mouth pressed soft kisses along my back. Every inch of me was ablaze. "Put your hands against the wall."

"Why?" I asked, but then his tongue swept across my folds and ass, then back again as he sucked on that little bundle of nerves. I cried out in pure bliss. He knocked my legs wider apart and then came to his knees beneath me, his mouth consuming me.

Oh, great kings, this man knew exactly what he was doing, unlike the previous man I went to who attempted to pleasure me with his fingers and mouth.

His teeth nibbled against my clit while two fingers plunged in and out of me at a punishing pace. Everything around me disappeared. It was only me and him.

"Come for me, Wildcat. Ride my tongue the way I know you can." His palm smacked across my ass cheek as I clenched down around him. A moan of pleasure escaped me as my orgasm ripped through me, and I writhed against him.

As he came closer to me, I noticed his lips were glossy and swollen. His tongue darted out to clean it, and with a smile, he said, "I was right. You taste as sweet as you smell."

I stared into his eyes, and something was wrong. Normally, I feel overwhelming guilt being with another man—well, that other man—but this time, it felt…it felt right. I scrambled to get dressed, giving him a swift apology on the way out.

The door slammed behind me. I never want to remember this night again.

****

Jaxx

Today was the worst possible morning to be on my list. After being left stranded last night by that woman, then chased by the other, who asked me why I hadn't killed her. How was I supposed to know the woman I had in my room was the same that fucked over this client? A droplet of blood slides down from his busted lip as I raise my fists back further.

"I'm sorry, Jaxx. He just left." I can smell the fear; savoring it. It fuels my powers and strengthens them.

"You had one job, just like your ancestors before." My victim's warm chocolate eyes wavered in a face carved from midnight. "He left months ago with a woman."

I furrow my brows. "What woman?" I say,

bringing him to his feet with my hand still wrapped tightly around the collar of his blouse.

"She had hair like honey and eyes like sapphires, and she was exquisitely beautiful." A woman has entered my baby brother's life. I should have known that time would come.

"Who else was with them? Was she a witch?"

"No, she was just a princess from one of the other kingdoms."

"A princess, you say?" I look around for the pitiful excuse for a home. Green and black mold stains the deteriorating stone walls, while the rusted galvanized rooftop sags inward. A single storm will make this house crumble. Letting him fall to the hardened floor, I brush loose strands from my face.

"I will spare you the death you deserve only because your greatest grandmother kept her word. Not a word of this to anyone." Still cowering on the floor, he nods as I push through the splintered door. Approaching my horse, I mount it with ease.

"Where to, boss?" Jon, my second and torture expert, asks from his horse beside me.

Pulling my black hood up over my tied-back charcoal hair, I answer, "Tell me, Jon, do you know about a foreign princess with hair like honey and eyes the color of gems?" I pull my black mask up to cover my face below my nose.

"Sounds like the lost Princess of Thornwharf." Lost princess, he says? It is more like an enchanter. In all my years watching over my baby brother, I have never once seen or heard about him taking a woman for his own. I thought he would be safe from that.

"To Thornwharf we go. Have Guss and Carlyle

scout ahead. I need to have a conversation with this princess." The sinister laughter leaving Jon tells me he understands exactly what I mean. Torture her for information, fuck her, then kill her.

As we ride toward our destination, I think about the last time I saw him. It was just eight months ago when he was serving as a guard for the Prince of Greveil, an honorable position. One night, he went on a mission. I got word of Supreme Leader Rai's movements across the Great Sea. I should have intervened and made myself known to him.

I almost did one night a decade ago when he was patrolling through the village.

The rain was soft, a light sprinkle as the White Sun reached its highest peak. His back was to me as I kept two wings span lengths from him. He carried double blades strapped to his sides. I rarely have ever seen him use them.

Stopping, he looks over his shoulder as I disappear behind a house. Peeking around the corner, I notice he is gone.

"Who the fuck are you, and why are you following me?" The sharp tips of his blades press against my neck.

"Just trying to get home," I innocently say.

"Let me escort you the rest of the way." I cannot help but feel pride in how strong he has become. The power illuminated off him. And he does not even know the extent of it yet.

"That isn't necessary," I say as he lowers his weapons. "It's exactly right here."

After finding out my brother was an honorable man, I made something of myself after two hundred and forty-six years of living in the shadows like a wraith in the night. The one lesson I learned after the Dragon War ended was that mortals are selfish. I have seen the poor die from starvation when a rich man could have fed that family and theirs for many years.

Instead of exposing myself fully, I built a group of honorable men who would serve me so we could serve the impoverished. It is something I know our parents would approve of.

Thundering through the forest, my hidden wings beg me to release them. It has been a while since I last took a flight. My boys don't know what I truly am. I like to keep it that way. There is no need for rumors of another Ashana flying around.

The Evergreens drip with the de-thawing frost that comes at the end of winter. Warmer weather will come soon. As night falls, the temperature drops, but we continue ahead through the heavily traveled path used by merchants across kingdoms. I am not sure how long we will ride for, but the one thing about us, or me, is I don't sleep.

When I do, that is when they come. Memories of my failure. The sword pierced my father through. The pain is too much, the images too real. A shiver runs down my spine at the memory of what it smelled like.

The halting of Jon's horses makes me pull on the reins hard. Ironhide's front legs kick in the air as he neighs in protest. "What's the problem?"

"Dead body."

"Walk around it." Those bright blue irises look eerily at me.

"It's Guss." Dismounting from my horse, I walk past Jon as he follows my lead, approaching the dead body. Kneeling, I see the pool of crimson leaking from his slit throat.

"Where are the rest of the men?"

"They should be with hi-" The whizzing of arrows, the striking of a dagger to a neck, and the smell of blood—my senses go crazy. Turning, I see Jon hit the ground, choking on his blood.

"Ambush." Running to Ironhide, I mount him in one leap, charging forward. A group of ten men come out from the trees, stopping us in our tracks. I am knocked from my saddle but catch myself before face-planting the ground. "Big mistake, boys."

"Boys?" The soldiers split when a woman with white hair, silver tattoos of swirls, and midnight-colored skin approaches me. Dressed in all white, except for green clusters on her cuff links. She wields a golden staff.

"Forgive me. I don't take pity on women."

"We don't need pity from you, Hooded Mercenary. Before we imprison you for your crimes against the crown, do you have any last requests?" It has been a while since my last fight, and this should be fun.

"What makes you thin-" I don't see it before it pricks my neck. My tongue swells, and my vision blurs. "How did you-"

"We know what you are—a demon. You think I would not come after you without doing my research first?" As she approaches me, I try to use my powers to take flight, but I am paralyzed. "Sleep well, demon. For tomorrow will be your last." My world becomes consumed by darkness.

The rough, icy surface of the ground sends ice shards through my body. Snapping awake, the taste of ash is in my mouth. Looking around, I notice rows of vertical iron bars surrounding me. Torches, mounted to the stone wall of a barren room, give a dim ambiance.

"You're awake." The voice of the white-haired woman I met carries in the small room.

"Where am I?" was not the first question I meant to ask. Gripping the iron bars, I try to pull them out of their sockets, but I am met with resistance and a feeling of dizziness.

"Careful, demon. The serum is still running its course through your veins." Serum? What is she talking about? "My name is Alma. I am the queen's guard and acting authority over the three territories."

"Nice to meet you. Now, I warn you to let me out before you find your entrails outside your body." The glow of the fire shimmers around her as she approaches me, unafraid.

"You are no threat with that serum running through your veins."

"Tell me, Alma, why do you have me caged like some common criminal?"

"Because you are."

"Stealing from the rich to ensure the poor survive hardly seems like a crime."

"And you are a demon." Her intense stare has me heated with intrigue.

"What kind of magic did you use to suppress my supposed demonic powers?" I am genuinely curious because if there is magic that can do that, then Calian and I will be more vulnerable than I feared.

"Dragon's blood," she plainly states.

"And pray tell what manner of beast would allow themselves to be drained?"

"That is no concern of yours."

"So mysterious. Tell me..." I pause, rubbing the stubble on my chin. "...does your queen know about this? What about her lover?"

"You mean her husband." Little brother got himself a mate. "I will not have you insult my queen and breathe another second."

"Ah, but you cannot kill me. Otherwise, I would already be dead." She stiffens. "I suspect your queen wants to have a conversation with me, which is why my head is still on my shoulders." Silence and a slight glance to the side. "I will speak with her mate, Ashana, and only him."

"You are in no position to bargain with me."

"And you are in way over your head." I smell something dark coming from her. Tasting like the venom of a serpent as it pierces your flesh. She turns to leave. "Could you please bring me something fresh to eat? I am dreadfully famished."

The metal door slams, and I hear a click as the lock turns. Today, I got to see my baby brother. What a reunion this will be.

Chapter Two

Abbygale

Tossing my clothes to the side, I sink into the warm bath, waiting for me when I get home just before dawn. I scrubbed quickly, acting like the soap would wash away tonight's activities. My pussy still throbbed with the memory of his lips pressed against it. Who was he? It does not matter now, and I will never see him again.

After drying, I quickly get dressed in a simple evening gown, my robe, and strap at least one blade to my side. If the past year has taught me anything, it is that just because there are rotating guards does not mean this place is impenetrable. I pass by the small table beside my bed and see a folded envelope with the rose symbol on it.

"Dear Abbygale,

I need your aid at Thornwharf. We intend to bring in a known criminal, and it would do me a great honor to go with us during the interrogations. If anything, we can spar each other again. See you in three days.

Clover."

Summoned like a commoner. One of these days I will escape court life. Find a house made from trees. Maybe even grow some flowers. A verbal laugh left me at the delusion I had just presented to myself. I tossed the paper onto the bed, then left my room. I had to keep up with the tradition of seeing him.

Our tombs were out in the vast courtyard at the far back of the castle. Mother and Father's ashes were in the royal temple, but they were not who I came to see each night. I loved my parents dearly, but I knew they would pass on eventually. A chill raised up my spine as I settled in front of Tristian's statue. The words carved under the replica of his boots: 'Here lies Tristian, loyal, brave, and true.'

The stone carver did an amazing job matching the description I gave him. They had asked me since my sister was off getting married and becoming queen of Orion. They gave me that excuse, but I suspect it was because they all knew I was the woman he had loved last.

"It does not get any easier, you know. Going every day without you here." I run my hand over the smooth stone surface of what was supposed to be his right cheek. I come out here every chance I can to talk to him. Unsure if he can hear me or not. There is not much I know about the afterlife of the Realm of Immorteum, but at least he does not have to deal with the fucked up parts of life anymore.

"She is married, you know. And they plan to make me an aunt soon. Kaleigh keeps saying it will happen after the war ends and we are officially at peace, but I think it will happen sooner than she thinks." I sigh; the guilt I feel for his death weighs on me every day. And I swore to never love another the way I loved him.

When I ventured out that night to take another man into my bed, I was trying to test myself to see if I could move on. But when he tried to kiss me, to touch me, it made me feel sick to my stomach with guilt. I only let him touch me as a way of punishing myself, and it was a terrible experience. After hearing he was married a few hours later, I was even more upset. My fingers trailed over the scar on my forearm from the first attempt I made to shut off the pain.

That is all I was trying to do. I imagine that is what any person dealing with grief wants. Numb the guilt, fill the hole in your heart with ale, sex, and aphrodisiacs. The last I had never tried nor wanted to. Being self-aware of my surroundings is a part of my nature now. If anyone tried to take an attempt on my life, I would be ready for them.

Flashes of the dragon shifter, or man with dragon wings, unsure what he truly was, come to mind. He had threatened me with his flames but did not act on them. It made me curious why he had hidden them. I know Calian is the son of a god, but I thought he was the only one in all Dalaria. But those were not my only questions for this man. Why had I been so drawn to him I allowed myself to be completely naked? Dropping my guard for even a few moments, as blissful as they were, was a foolish move to make.

"I'm sorry," I whispered, unsure if it was to my lost love or to myself.

I wipe a stray tear away. There was no time for crying.

"Would you mind if I joined you?" Kaleigh asked. I nodded, and she took her seat beside me. "I miss him too."

Not like I do. That is what I wanted to say, but I know he was her best friend and lover before Rowland rolled into our lives.

"Yeah," I muttered.

"It has been four months, Abby. We still have not talked about it." I looked away from her, not wanting to acknowledge that fact. "You haven't properly grieved yet."

"Yeah, well, we have been prepping for another war, remember? We prioritize Orion and Zoldir above everything else, and now Princess Clover and all the dragon souls are our mission. And who are you to say what is proper or not about the grieving process? I don't see you taking a second away from your new husband to even memorialize Tristian."

"Watch your tone, and the court politics is not your responsibility; I'm the queen," she argued. I faced away from her. She is matured so much in the last four months, and I know I should not hold her being some magical fucking queen with a husband against her, but—I am envious of her successful conclusion.

I toyed with a white rose lying atop the headstone. "You know, when we got separated in the Snow Forest before Rowland showed up, Tristian found a white rose still blooming, and although he pricked his finger to get it for me, that was the moment we went from friends to lovers—our first kiss."

She smiled. "Wow."

I blinked. "What?"

Kaleigh came and interlaced her fingers with mine. "That's the first time you've spoken to me about him without accusing me of killing him."

I scoffed and jerked away from her. "You are a selfish bitch."

"Excuse me?" She appeared taken aback.

I looked at her, astonished that she did not seem to realize just how fucking ignorant and insensitive she has become to mine and his memory. "You got him killed. Letting him join you on a quest you knew was dangerous. His blood is on your hands and there is not anything you can change about that. Next time you want to talk to me about him or judge me on the way I am handling his death, look at yourself in the mirror first."

Her blue eyes rimmed with tears, but they would never fall—not in front of me or for me. My big sister was just as stubborn as I was. "You truly hate me? After everything I have had to do to ensure Orion and our people are safe? To make sure you had a future?"

"Future? What future? I am not the heir. The second-born never takes the throne because the first always has children to take over when they die."

"Is that what you want, then? For me to name you my heir?"

I scoffed, shaking my head from side to side. "If you knew me as well as you think you do, you would understand that I don't give a fuck about ruling. I am a soldier."

"I should have never let you come with me on that quest to find Rowland. It darkened your soul and erased everything that made you want to be queen. Abby, sister, please let us make amends so we can do this together." She reached for my hands, but I stepped away from her.

"No. I will not be queen. A lot has changed. When Dalaria is finally at peace, you will never see me in this god forsaken place again." I exit, saying one last thing over my shoulder, "I am heading to Thornwharf. If you need me, well, don't."

****

"I know you asked me to arrive in three days, but I had to get out of Orion," I explained to Clover as I dropped my pack on the bed in the guest chambers. The floral wall paint makes me feel like vomiting. With my arms crossed over my chest, I faced her. "Please, don't make me go back. Kaleigh is being a real bitch."

Clover raised a brow, then sighed. "You should be more appreciative of your sister. You both have been through a lot in your young lives. She just wants what is best."

"Isn't that what your mother told you when she was cutting your skin?" I regretted saying that the moment my words slipped from my mouth. Clover visibly flinched with pain. "I should not have said that my sister may be a prude pain in my ass, but she is nothing like your mother. Forgive me?"

"Of course. All I was trying to say was to remember that your sister had to become queen sooner than she wanted to. You all fought in a war that you never thought would happen and now are going to be thrust into another. Your sister may mother you sometimes, but it's only because she is doing what she knows best."

"Annoy the hell out of me?" I asked, then smirked.

"Protect her baby sister. Only now does she know you can take care of yourself. I imagine it must be difficult to accept that," she explained, and I thought about it.

Of course, Kaleigh had looked out for me all my life. Helping to feed me before I knew how to eat with my hands. She was there every night, reading to me as soon as she could put words into sentences. Guilt rushed through me at my last encounter with her.

"Thanks, Clover."

"No need. Rest. I have my queen's guard out searching for the criminal." She approached the door and then looked over her shoulder to say, "I want you to know that your secret is safe with me."

Secret? "What? I don't have any secrets."

It was time to meet in the throne hall since we had captured the prisoner early last night. I seethed my daggers to my sides, took one long look at myself in the looking glass, and then made my way to the throne room. Calian and Clover were deep in conversation the moment I entered. Thank the gods for that.

"Alma said it was an easy capture," Clover said. While I stood to her right as she told Calian about her first impression of his long-lost magical brother.

I did not like the pretty princess from the other side of the Great Sea at first, but when she became a badass goddess, then my opinions changed. She has become what I might call a friend. If anything, she is an excellent sparring partner.

"Maybe he'll break easily," Calian commented. He is angry, judging by his puffed-out chest and persistent scowl. Learning about another sibling who never tried to reach out to me might have made me feel angry.

But then again, I don't think I want another one.

The doors creaked open, and the air in the room was suddenly hot. Clover looked at me, a small smile playing at the corner of her lips, before she focused her attention on the doorway. I blinked three times, momentarily confused by why she was playing games. A heartbeat later, my mouth felt dry, the taste of ash filled my mouth, and I instantly became ensnared in his dark green gaze. Clover's last words played on repeat.

"Your secrets are safe with me."

Chapter Three

Jaxx

Iron binds my wrists together as I am walked out of the dungeon. The magic used has made all my powers disappear completely.

I have never felt so weak before. Not since the day my parents died.

The stone staircase leads up to another metal door. When opened, it flows into a narrow hall. The marbled floor is white and connects to large floral covered walls. They almost seem lifelike with the twisting and turning of each prickled vine. Each decorated with fresh flowers.

"Your queen must love the gardens," I say to Alma. In the light of the High Sun, I take in the full beauty of her. The silver tattoos I saw before were more detailed with swirls and sigils, reminding me of the times when all the gods lived with the humans.

Down the hall, we make our way through various corners, passing servants and other doors that hold the secrets of this palace. Despite my loss of magic, I could still fight my way out of it. If only these damn iron chains were not binding me.

As we approach two posted soldiers, there is an entrance with no doors. To my surprise, we turn and three individuals greet us as they converse at the center.

The room goes silent, and all eyes turn to me as I enter.

"Don't stop the party on my account." I smirk. "On second thought, I believe the party has just begun." I feel the bone tips of my wings dragging slightly across the tiled floor.

Cal's dark green eyes alight at the sight of me. "Hello, brother."

"Kneel." Following Alma's command, her staff swiftly strikes the back of my knees, forcing me to kneel before the queen. With a hard thud, I feel the pain of my curved bones hitting the floor.

"I like it rough, but you could at least buy me a drink first." I see her move to strike me, but the brown-haired woman moves quickly, gripping her wrist.

"I don't think it is wise to strike him while he is defenseless." I meet her eyes, and something is familiar about her. Her scent? Those ocean-blue eyes?

"Jaxx," the woman with honey-colored hair calls my attention to her. "Do you know why you are in chains?"

"Because your guard attacked, drugged, and kidnapped me." I gesture my head toward the white-haired warrior.

"You are in chains because you are a criminal." She takes a step closer, and I watch as Cal stays in his spot, still assessing me. "I would like to remove those chains, but first you must give me your word you won't cause problems or flee."

"I rarely make deals with royal scum, but," —I pause, looking at Cal— "for the sake of my baby brother, I will give you my word."

As Alma approaches me, I add a condition. "I want her to do it." I point at the woman with the auburn-colored hair. In the light streaming through the windows, I can see the faintest streaks of gold mixed in.

Reluctantly, she grabs the keys as I am pulled to my feet. I tower a foot or two over her. Those pools of dark blue show curiosity and a hint of danger. She smells of lilac and desire. Now I know exactly where I met her.

"Beautiful." It slips out low enough for only her to hear. Her eyes travel to my lips, then back up to my eyes. Without breaking eye contact, she unlocks my wrists. Her knuckles brush my hand slightly and sent a pulse through me. As I'm handed the chains, I grip her wrists and pull her into me. I press my chest against her back, wrap a hand around her slender neck, and pin her arms. "I still remember the taste of you on my tongue, princess."

I can feel the pulse in her neck increase as I press my lips to it. She remembers me.

"Halt," the queen orders as the guards charge toward me. "You went back on your word."

"As your guard put it earlier, I am a criminal. Now let me go, or I snap her neck." None of them move and it confuses me until I am suddenly on my back with a dagger at my throat. Two blue flames peering down at me. "Aren't you a wildcat?"

"If you think I won't slit you from ear to ear, you are mistaken," she warns and I cannot help that my cock responds by twitching. I have been with plenty of human women before, but none has been as intriguing as this one. She is acting as if we have not met prior to now. A silent plea for my silence dances in her eyes.

I give her a wink, then hold my hands up in surrender.

"Abby, I think you have proven your point," the queen said.

"Are we going to have a problem, Jaxx?" Abby asks. I have never wanted to fight and fuck someone so badly before.

As she removes the dagger slowly, I lean up to whisper in her ear, "I usually like my women under me, as you well know, but I can make an exception for you." My tongue trails along her cheek. She lets out a breathy moan before heat comes across my face. "Feisty and violent."

"You are no brother of mine." Cal's words cut through the heat developing between me and Abby. We get to our feet. "Treat Abbygale Orion with respect, for she is a princess," Cal proclaimed.

Oh, my dear brother, ever the gentleman. "Beg pardon, princess." I feign a bow.

"Enough," the queen's commanding tone rings out. "My name is Chloe. You are here because we received word that you know the location of the shadow magic we need to destroy the Dark Wizard."

My gaze shifts from Abby to Chloe. "I might know the information you seek." If they want to take down the Dark Wizard, they better offer me more than my freedom. Cal may be my blood, but we are not family. Not like we should have been.

"Tell us," Cal snarls.

"So primal. I thought when you finally fucked a whore, you would not be so angry." I prepare for an assault from Cal, but it is not his hand who is lifting me in the air. In a shimmering light of gold, Chloe has pure white wings, and her sapphire-colored eyes are now white.

"You will not insult him," she warns.

"Is not this a twist? My, my, you did not just fuck a royal whore. You fucked a goddess. I must say that I am pro—" She throws me into the wall. I hear the crunch of my wings as my breath catches on impact. The flash of that dreaded day hits me with the faint smell of smoke.

"You understand that you have no power here. Whether you agree to give that information up willingly or not, we will get it out of you." Chloe's threats send a tremor of fear through me. I am weak without my powers, but even if I had them, I would not stand a chance against a goddess. "Believe me when I say this, the methods of torture are quite familiar to me."

Getting to my feet, I spit blood onto the ground. "It won't be easy to get the materials required for the spell," I state.

"What spell?" Cal asks.

"You need magic to destroy magic." I slowly walk over to them. "To create the dagger of Vertumnus, we need elements from each species of dragon."

"Why does it have to be dragons?" Abby asks.

"Because the Dark Wizard committed the ultimate sin to become who he is today," I answer. All three exchange glances. "He was not always a murderous bastard. He was a human once upon a time.

"Before the war started, he was an advisor to one of the human kings. An adversary between dragons, elves, and humans. Somewhere along the way, he lost his position. Like any typical pathetic human, he sought revenge. He searched the deepest, darkest parts of the world and found the colony of Shadow Dragons. They all became excellent friends and thus began the Dragon

Wars."

"What was the ultimate sin?" Abby asks.

"Killing our father. Tika, God of Dragons." I have not told that story to anyone. There is more to it, but it is too painful to speak about. They will never know; Cal will never know the pain of losing them. Watching them get murdered right before my eyes.

"What are the ingredients?" Cal asks, avoiding my stare.

"Blood from each leader of every colony. Ice, fire, earth, nurture, and shadow," I answer.

Silence slices through the air. A coldness takes over the room.

"Alma…" I watch as the queen's guard approaches her. "Contact Queen Kaleigh, I need them to wait to free the souls. Tell her why and that we will once we head back."

"Yes, Your Majesty." Alma leaves and I watch as a wicked grin comes across her smooth skin and a flash of black crosses over the whites of her eyes.

"Are you sure you can trust her?" I state. Knowing they would not trust me over her.

"I would trust her with my life," Chloe states, making me roll my eyes at the cliche response.

"We just got here and now we are heading back?" Abby asks. For a princess, she is very unorthodox.

"Your sister is heading to the temple to free those souls. If we are not there to get the blood, then we will have to travel around the entire world and we don't have that kind of time. Cal does not have that kind of time." At the mention of my brother, I snap out of my daze.

"What's wrong?" I ask.

"Nothing that you should concern yourself with," Cal says. "How do we know he isn't lying?" Cal points an accusatory finger toward me.

"You hurt me." I feign a gasp, clutching my chest. "What reason would I have to lie to you? I want revenge for our parents' murder."

"I can tell he isn't lying," Chloe states. I have heard and seen my father's god-like power, but never a goddess. And I am curious to find out which one she is. Clearly reincarnated.

"Thank you, Chloe," I comment. Cal married a smart one.

"We should contact Azula," Abby states. Another member of this little group. I am slowly becoming more curious about this blue-eyed princess. Her mouth moves freely without fear of rejection or correction. I admire her spirit, and it incites me to get to know her better.

"For now, we need to rest and eat. Tomorrow, we can go back to the docks," Chloe states.

"Should this be an opportune time to mention the other ingredients?" They all shoot daggers at me. As if my voice offends them. "You need to retrieve the dagger itself. Last I heard, some queen up north has possession of it."

"You bastard." Cal charges toward me, but Chloe stops him. He has a short temper. Something feels off about that. Last I saw, he had a cool head on his shoulders.

"Queen Iliana has received the weapon we need to kill the Dark Wizard? How do you know this?" Chloe asks.

"Well, Your Majesty, I have been the Hooded Mercenary for over a decade. My many transactions with royal donors, I have learned that drunks give up more than their coin." I pause, shifting my gaze to Abby, who seems unaffected by me at all. "Secrets can be just as heavy as money." I admire her from head to toe. She narrows her eyes at me, gripping the hilt of her blades at her waist in warning. I lick my lips, expecting the start of something new.

"Chloe, are you seriously going to believe him?" Cal hates me. Good, he needs to hate me. As much as I would love to form some kind of bond with him, it would make him a weakness. I learned from my father what having a weakness means. My baby brother has one. Chloe is not immune to being killed, regardless of her status as a goddess. If you find out which one she is.

"I believed you after you kidnapped me," Chloe states. Not so honorable, baby brother.

"That was different," he says defensively.

"Was it, Cal? Because I seem to remember after you kidnapped me, you kissed me, then I found myself chained to a wall. Should I remind you of that?" Much respect for this goddess. Calling out my baby brother should make me angry, but it just amuses me.

"Fine, but I warn you, Jaxx. You betray us and I will take a dragon bone dagger and stab you in the heart." He steps forward as if to ensure I know how serious he is.

"So territorial. Makes me wonder how much of you is mortal." I move closer to him. "And how much is the dragon."

"Thank you for your cooperation, Jaxx. I will have my guards escort you out," Chloe states. They cannot get rid of me that easily.

"Before I go, I should warn you that your precious

guard has concocted some type of serum that suppresses the powers of an Ashana. She is not to be trusted."

"Liar." Cal's brows furrow in fury.

"Fine. Don't believe me. But if the fact that a little woman can pin me down does not back up my statement, then I don't know what will. I don't have any of my powers, except I still have my wings." The anger is difficult to hide, but my patience is running thin. I dislike being accused of lying.

"We will look into it, thank you," Chloe states. "Now, please get out of my throne room before I have you tossed out."

"As you wish, Your Majesty." I feign another bow, stealing a glance at Abby before exiting. They cannot get rid of me that easily. Especially that delicious-looking princess. I will not be far behind them when they leave.

It is not about protecting my baby brother. This is about avenging the murder of my mother and father. I will thrust that dagger through the heart of the wizard, even if it kills me to do so.

Chapter Four

Abbygale

Escorting duty.

That is what I am to all these people. Someone to use for tedious tasks. That happens when you're not the direct heir. Not that I mind the less pressure of my title.

But ensuring an egotistical dragon shifting demigod leaves without issue? Now that is something I am delighting in.

I tugged on his thick biceps, marching him further out of the castle. His wings drag across the floor, as if he had no strength to lift them and does not mind the screeching sound ripping down the narrow halls.

"Can't you put those away?" I snap.

"Sorry, wildcat, no can do. I am not like my baby brother, who hides his true form once revealed," he responds, and I roll my eyes at him. "Besides, you wouldn't be able to see how big I am—my wingspan, that is."

I suck my teeth at that and then stop. Turning toward him, I grip his left wing by the bone, lifting it.

"Control them, or I cut it off," I threaten.

He growls, prowling toward me like a predator, but I don't back down. We are face to face and I realize I have let go of his wing. "Do that again, and there will be consequences."

His dark green eyes look at me, moving back and forth as his warning seeps into me.

"I don't fear you, Ashana." The soft whisper might be a contradiction because I know if he had access to his powers, he could kill me.

"How long are you going to pretend that you don't know me?" he asks, a smirk playing along his lips. I don't answer him because I am not entirely sure how to feel about this man. He is a criminal but also, something about him makes me want to take him to my bed and let him bring me to bliss repeatedly. I shake those thoughts out of my head. "You still owe me, princess."

"I owe you nothing."

"Oh, really? Shall I remind you I stood in my room, which I paid for, naked, hard, and cold, with no one to warm my cock? And that I had just given you the best orgasm of your entire life?"

"Shut up," I snap.

"Why? Afraid your friends will know you have been converting with a criminal?"

"No…it…just. Oh, will you just leave it alone? We are to never speak of that night, ever again." I point my blade at him to add to the threat, knowing it would not do much good.

Lifting his hands, the chain between them rattles and he asks, "Can you remove these? Unless you would rather I keep them on while I let you use me. Again."

He winks and I scoff before letting the iron fall to the floor. We don't move. Our breaths mingle between us. And my heart races as my core stirs. I have not felt this since—the ground quakes, breaking our bubble—thank the kings.

My body hits the floor. Jaxx's body is on top of mine, his large wings protecting us from the falling rumble crumbling from the ceiling. "Hold on to me!"

I blink twice and wrap my body around his, not looking away from his shimmering eyes. He smirks as the taste of ash fills my mouth and jerks my body sideways. I feel the cool, crisp grass from the castle grounds under me and a grumble of complaints on my insides. Quickly rolling over, I empty the contents of my stomach and Jaxx holds my braids out of the way while rubbing my back. "What...the fuck just happened?"

"I saved your life. No need to thank me." I swat his hand away and stand, looking at the remnants of the fortress of Thornwharf. "Look, you actually did well for your first time being teleported."

I scan the rubble, looking for Chloe and Calian. Anyone else could have made it out.

"Help me!" I see a hand sticking out. Ignoring Jaxx's protest, I race over and grip a woman's hand. I see her brown eyes widen with fear, her face coated in dust, and her arm bleeding. I grip the edge of the rocks and move the ones I can lift.

One after the other until I finally get her freed. But then something remains. It is big enough to cover her from chest to waist. Blood seeps from the corners of her mouth, and I hear her choking. "Please, save me."

"Hang on. I can get you out." I bend my knees, using all the strength I can muster, and pull up, but nothing happens. As I scan my surroundings for additional help, no one comes into view. Once again, I attempt. And again. Until I fall backward. I roll up my sleeves, close my eyes, and calm myself. *Please, give me the strength.* I feel it lifting. My body burns in pain with each movement I make. But I don't give up. When it finally moves completely from her torso, I lean down, cradle her, and drag her to the safety of the grass.

"There, you're safe—" I look over and see nothing of the light left in her brown eyes. The hope of seeing me helping her has vanished. I press two fingers to her neck, praying for a pulse, but feel nothing. "No. No. I saved you. You cannot leave me. I made it in time. No!"

I punch my fist in her chest. Something I have seen royal healers do to bring a dead soldier back to life. "Please, come back." My voice cracks. I keep going until a thick hand wraps around my wrist, halting me. Two green eyes filled with sympathy meet mine. Thick arms pull me in for a warm embrace and his scent fills my nose, bringing me back to my senses. "You did your best, Wildcat."

I push away, jumping to my feet and wiping the dust from my clothes. "Well, I guess my best wasn't good enough."

"Jaxx, Abby, are you okay?" Chloe's voice breaks my concentration, and I meet up with her. She reaches for my arms. "Not my blood."

She nods. "We must get to Greveil. Your sister has freed the souls, and Prince Eli is friends with the prince of Shulong. He will have the answers we need to ensure we receive the dagger."

I searched for Calian but could not find him anywhere. "Where is Cal?"

Chloe's eyes turn down. "Rai's magic was too powerful. My mate has disappeared into the shadows of darkness. We must hurry."

Chapter Five

Jaxx

Dark fluids from my enemies coat my skin, but I don't care. I relish in the feel of my blades cutting through their flesh and bone. What makes this moment even better is the sight of the beautiful woman fighting next to me. Each throw of her steel daggers reaches its target with a deadly accuracy. When we arrived at Greveil, Eli was initially welcoming until he was a dumbass and threatened a goddess. After she burned his cock off, his guards rushed in, alerting us of Rai's attack on the fortress.

"That makes thirteen, Dragonboy." The fierce nature of this woman ignites something new inside of me. A fire that was never there until now. I am stunned for a moment as I watch her take down three more monsters, each twice as tall as her, and at least ten times as strong. But she does not back down. Does not cower in fear. She is a survivor, like me.

"Jaxx," she yells just as the steel of one of her daggers flies past my face before connecting with the head of an Orc behind me. She comes running up to me, her breath heavy with the fight. Kneeling, she plucks the dagger from the beast's head before giving me a stern look. "Pay attention."

"I would, but you are so damn distracting," I tease

with a wink. Earning an eye roll along with a smirk. We look around. I notice Emnera flying toward us before landing.

"We need to leave," she commands. I look toward Abby.

"You want us to stop fighting? What about these innocent villagers?" the princess retorts.

"Abby, please." Abbygale is right. Of course, it would be immoral to leave these defenseless people to fight these beasts. "We could combine our powers, but that could also be a major risk," I suggest.

I see her head fall with grief. "No, I don't want to leave the innocents to be slaughtered, but," —she looks at us again— "the bigger mission is more important."

"And what, I am just supposed to accept that? What are they to you? Collateral damage?" Abby's tone rises with her anger. Only she is brave enough to challenge a goddess and survive. But Emnera is not a typical goddess.

"My opinion aligns with hers," I stated, gesturing towards Abby.

"That isn't wise," Emnera said. I can tell she is not comfortable using her powers with the potential damage it could do. More shouts from soldiers, screams from widows and orphans fill my ears and fuel my anger.

"Do you hear that?" I can hear the anger in my tone, feel my eyes narrow in fury. "That is the sound of recent widows. They will slaughter those who don't yield. We can help them."

I can see the inner turmoil with which she is dealing. What choice is the correct one? What choice will bring us closer to getting Cal back? I flex my wings, preparing to make my choice, when I hear screeches from above. Instantly, we all look up and see black shadows attacking Ziran.

The same ones I witnessed my parents' murder. A memory of the day flashes before my eyes. My mother's screams of pain echo in my ears as the heat of the fire burns the flesh from her bones while I could not move. Unable to save her from her death.

"We need to help her." I yell. Before she says a word of protest, I take flight. My swords ignited with dragon fire. You will not take her. Not again. Not today.

The closer I get, the faster my heart beats with the anticipation of killing. My eyes zero in on the first beasts clawing at Ziran's neck. Her crimson blood coats her shimmering emerald scales. Stabbing both blades into the sides of the Shadow Dragon, it loosens its grip on Ziran while screeching out its pain.

"Burn, you bastard. Burn for all your sins!" It cranes its shadowed neck so it can look at me before opening its jaws to shoot its flames of black toward me. Forming an X with my swords, I block its attack. Steadying myself, I erect my wings so I can balance myself—the whip of a tail comes across my back, sending bolts of sharp pain tingling through my body.

"Fuck." Moving slightly higher, I gaze down at my opponent. "You shouldn't have done that." Using my teleportation power, I move fast and slice even faster. Relentless with my assault, I feel my inner fire fueling the flames on my blades. Increasing the heat until the metal melts.

When my blades become nothing but melted steel, I toss them aside. For a split second, Ziran catches my eye. She is still fighting off two more. *Why doesn't Emnera help?*

I will not stop there. I continue, one after the next. With nothing but blades made from my fire, I continue cutting and slicing until the she-dragon is free. Turning around, I come eye to eye with the biggest one. Its hollow eyes staring into my soul. I see the faintest light of a soul trying to escape the hollowed-out eye sockets. For a moment, we both float there. Having a silent conversation, neither of us knows what words to use.

With a shake of its head, it leaves without so much as a flicker of a flame to attack me. Instantly, a bright light came from behind me, burning through the last of the Shadow Dragons. Turning, I see her. The white of her light shrinks as she rings her powers back in.

"You helped, after all." Emnera shoots past me, ignoring my presence completely. My eyes follow her as I see her holding onto the very injured green dragon.

"Help me land her!" Emnera shouts over the wind. I look up—Ziran's wings are shredded, barely holding her aloft. My chest tightens with helpless grief. Emnera takes her left flank; I move to her right. Together, we ease her down, struggling under her immense weight.

She's too heavy. My arms burn. My legs nearly buckle.

Then something changes.

A searing warmth spreads through me as Ziran's blood spills from a deep wound along her side, soaking into my skin. It's thick, hot—alive. I gasp, muscles surging with sudden strength not my own. The dragon's power seeps into me, filling my veins like fire.

I can bear her weight now.

I *am* strong enough.

I gently lower her shredded wing and move to place my hand over the fatal gash.

"Right now, I need bandages." I don't think the power to heal such a fatal wound exists. "Hurry."

"Here." My world becomes blurred by the noise that surrounds me. As soft hands meet mine, we press the white linens onto the wound, soaking up the crimson as it continues to flow. "Burn it."

"What?" Looking into the glazed dark blue of her eyes, I can see the worry on Abby's face.

"Burn the wound. It should stop the bleeding." I think for a moment before speaking. "Ziran." She groans in pain. "I am going to burn the wound. Are you ready?" Another groan, which does not sound like a protest, but also does not sound like approval. "Back up."

Once Abby gets the all-clear, I deliberately shut my eyes and direct my attention to her wound. Using my inner fire, strengthened by the dragon blood coating my skin, I let it flow from my core, down my arms, and into my hands, igniting the linens until they are ash. Her growls of pain fill my ears as silent tears fall from my eyes. I have not shed a tear since my parents' death, but Ziran is a dragon. I am the heir to the god of dragons; she is one of my subjects. My family.

As I increase my power, her wound closes, allowing time to heal itself until her beautiful skin is whole again. A faint pink scar is all that stays.

"You did it," Emnera's voice sounds, but I don't know if I can honestly believe what just happened. "You healed her. How did you do that?"

"I…" I have no words. No explanation for the power that just presented itself to me. Two hands cup my face. My eyes caught those two deep pools of blue, which I can only describe as the purest color and deepest shade, like the deepest part of the Great Sea.

"It's okay." I believe her. "You saved her life, which is the only thing that is important. Nothing else matters."

"Abby's right. We can figure out the rest later. For now, we need to leave," Emnera states. Getting to my feet, Abby releases her soft grip on me before walking to speak to Ziran.

"Jaxx," Emnera starts, "I sense your confusion and fear that this new power has brought on. You need not fear it. The power to heal is a gift from the gods, from your own father."

"Nothing my father ever gave me was a gift," I spat back. Not meaning to sound harsh. Emnera's look softened. Nothing pitiful but understanding. "I loved my father, but I have lived the last two centuries alone because of him."

"That was not your father's fault. It was Supreme Leader Rai. You know that." Her voice was soft. She was right, which is the reminder I needed why I am a part of this little group, anyway.

"I need to go clean up." A pitiful excuse, but one needed for me to get away from the empathy wanting to talk about feelings. Walking away from them, I hear Ziran murmur a thank you and I smirk at her over my shoulder.

The area we landed in is a tree line just beyond the village. The shouts of the siege have died down, telling me that the village has succumbed to its attackers. Abby must have followed the fight from the ground. I don't know what she sees in me to treat me with such undeserving kindness.

I come across a stream running just a few yards from the spot they are to wash the blood from my body and clothes. Stripping out of my tunic, I let the cool air kiss my skin as I sink my hands into the warm, clear water.

As the crimson and black leave my skin, I see the reflection of a man that I don't recognize anymore. Scrubbing my hands and arms clean, I cup a puddle into my hands and splash it on my face.

"Need a cloth?" My head snaps around at the voice. "Easy Dragonboy, I come in peace."

Standing, I look down at the chestnut-haired beauty approaching me. Her beautiful eyes trail down my body, sending a rush of desire through me. She steps closer, until we are toe to toe, and her breath is caressing my chest.

"I can help you. If you let me," she says seductively. Her challenging eyes investigate mine. As she reaches up to dry my chest, I grip her wrist in one hand, then wrap my arm around her waist, crushing her body to mine. Leaning my head in to whisper in her ear, my wet curls fall like a curtain over her.

"If I let you touch me before I have given you the pleasure of my touch, I would do you a disservice," I state soft enough so that my breath caresses her ear. I hear a gasp in response and her free hand grips the back of my neck.

"Maybe I want the pleasure of your touch, but you haven't earned it yet," she spats back before pushing me off and tossing the cloth at me. Turning on her heel, I watch as Abby marches back to camp. The cloth smells of her sweet scent. I will not ruin this by drying my skin. I decide to stuff it into my breeches pocket.

After cleaning all the blood off me, I put my tunic back on and tie my hair back into a bun. The cloth Abby gifted me is burning a hole in my pocket. Her scent is all around, driving me and dividing my attention.

Could she be….I mean, is she my…cannot be! If she were my mate, I would know, and why now? In my two-hundred and twenty-eight years of life, why would the gods bring her to me?

I shake the thoughts out of my mind as I make my way back to the group. Abby and Emnera are engaged in conversation with Ziran, who seems to be even better than before I left.

"Jaxx." Emnera draws the eyes of the others to me. I shoot a smirk and wink toward Abby, earning me her annoyed eye roll, and Ziran's eyes look admirably at me. She bows her head before speaking.

"Thank you, my King. I would not be alive without your healing touch." Ziran lowers her head before me as if asking me to touch her muzzle. It is a gesture of trust when a dragon lowers the head to another. The purest notion given to those they consider worthy of it.

I hesitate before placing my right palm upon her head, right between her eyes. She purrs in response.

"We need to get moving. Greveil is lost," states Emnera. "Eli has surrendered to their generals, and they have taken them prisoner."

"What about your traitorous guard?" I ask in a challenging tone, earning me a scornful look from Abby. *Oh, Princess, if you only knew who I truly am.*

"She is under the influence of shadow magic."

"The keyword being 'should.' And if she is not?"

Abby states. Emnera's expression changes to grief. An expression I know all too well.

"She will kill her," I answer for Emnera.

"Then we should get a move on. The faster we get this dagger, the faster all this bullshit shadow magic will be gone, and that bastard will become worm food." Abby walks toward a path in two parted Oaks.

I don't miss the opportunity to continue our conversation from earlier. Gripping her wrists as Emnera speaks with Ziran, I pull her closer to me. "Do you know how arousing you are when you give me orders?"

"Do not flatter yourself, Dragonboy. It was merely a suggestion." I look at my arm locked on her wrist. She could easily slip out of it if she wanted to.

"Look how at ease you are with my touch." Her eyes move to where our skin is touching. "Listen to how your heart pounds faster the closer I get to touching you with my lips." I lean in closer. "Your skin is heating as your sex drips for me."

A burning pain and the resounding sound of the slap come all at once across my face where Abby's free hand connected. Out of instinct, I let her go.

"Don't fucking touch me again." She snarls before walking away.

The disgusted look on her face does not overshadow the way I know her body reacts to me. Even if her heart and mind don't. I need her to hate me. The path of my vengeance will surely lead to my death, and that is a burden I will bear alone.

Chapter Six

Abbygale

I am not sure why I am letting him get to me.

He has a way of getting under my skin that no one has ever done, including Tristian. I let out a heavy sigh, feeling as though I was betraying the ghost of my former lover. I can barely remember him when Jaxx is near me. Everything about that wingman infuriates me but entices something deep inside I have never felt before. I sift through the underbrush for some dry pieces we can use for a fire. We must keep moving, but for tonight, we will get some sleep.

I feel for Chloe, who now wants to be called Emnera, as she has become a fully embraced goddess. Which is cool. I should be afraid of them. All these powerful beings, but it could be the stubbornness I was born with. There is nothing I find terrifying about any of them. Death does not scare me anymore. I am not sure if it ever did. Even when I had my first encounter with the leader of the Red Griffin Bandits.

Something that happened so long ago shaped me into the woman I am today. I will never tell my sister this, but her letting me go on that mission with her over a year ago is the best thing that could ever happen to me. I was naïve to the world. Defenseless, now look at me. Fighting side by side with demigods and goddesses.

The hair on the back of my neck rise, and I reach for the blade in my boot. I release a shallow breath before turning and throwing it at my target. Jaxx chuckles as he examines the plain hilt of my dagger. "Who taught you to be so deadly?"

I approached him, holding out my hand. "Give it back."

He arches a brow. "Ask nicely."

I shake my head. "Give it back, or the next one will land between your thighs."

He flips the blade, handing over the hilt while the sharpened end stays in his vice grip. I tug slightly and he does not even wince, just moves closer, and I feel my back hit the trunk of a tree. His free hand moves to just above me, and I lift my chin, puffing my chest out—completely unafraid. I watch as he assesses me from head to toe, as if I am the only person in the area. "You intrigue me, Wildcat. Something about you makes me want to crack down every brick you have built behind that beautiful bodice." He leans even closer, our noses brushing against one another. "But then again, it could be your tortuous scent that makes me want to taste every inch of your skin." My thighs rub together and my knees buckle slightly. "Hmm. Be careful, princess, your curiosity is showing."

Then he was gone, leaving me with a blood-soaked dagger and the chilly breeze hissing against the heat of my skin. I fall to my knees, clutching my chest to calm my racing heart. "Why does he affect me so?"

Later that night, I try to sleep but cannot. Looking up at the stars, I spoke, praying he can hear me. "Tristian," I whisper, "forgive me. I know I should still mourn you, but something about him is making me physically respond. But I cannot and will not betray your memory. No matter how I feel. No one could ever replace what we had. Or what I felt for you. I still love you. My heart still beats with the memory of you." I wipe a stray tear and then sigh.

I look over at Jaxx and then Emnera. They are fast asleep. I hear whimpering from Jaxx and glance over. His body is jerking, wings flexing, and sweat coats his brow. "No. Stop. Please, she is my mother." I crawl forward until I'm in front of him. His face is coated in fear. He's trapped in a nightmare, so I inch closer, hesitant. "Why did you do this?"

I move until our bodies press together, and I cup his face. "Jaxx, wake up." He keeps flinching without pause. "Please, it's just a dream." His hands grip my hips and then his nails dig into my clothes, tearing past the fabric until the sharp ends pierce my skin. I wince, but don't back away because I know what he is feeling. The panic of living the worst day of my life repeatedly not being able to save someone I loved. I press my forehead to his and whisper, "It's okay, Jaxx. Give me all your pain, all your suffering. I'll carry it—for both of us."

Blood drips down my hips and the pain intensifies as he flips me onto my back, pressing his body into mine. His wings flex, forming a protective barrier between us and the outside world. "Jaxx, wake up." Soft tears tumble down my cheeks. I move one hand to the back of his neck and press my lips to his. He stops moving. And then his tongue breaks the seam of my lips, and I let him in. I take on the pain, the guilt, the intensity of emotions he has and relish in it. I buck my hips up as his talons retract and the soft tips of his fingers replace them.

One hand moves slowly up my body, sliding over my chest as he palms my breast. His fingers tangle in my hair, jerking my head to the side before his lips find my neck and sucks it gently. His actions will leave a mark on my neck in the morning, but I don't care. I bite my lip to stifle a moan, even as his hard cock rubs against the seam of my pants. Fuck, I want him. And I hate myself for it. I buck my hips up when his hand lifts my shirt and rolls between us until I have him pinned with my dagger against his throat. His eyes are wide open, lips bruised and gloss with our kiss.

I clear my throat, "Good. You can take over the watch." I start to rise, but he holds me in place. I straddle him, gazing into his eyes.

"What did you do, Wildcat?" He looks at my blood coating his fingertips, then growls before looking at my hips. He presses his hands and I feel the burning pain of his fire igniting along my skin. My body sways as my stomach churns with unease at the smell of my flesh. Jaxx catches me as I fall back and my eyes drift close.

"Goodnight, Jaxx."

"Goodnight, Wildcat."

Chapter Seven

Jaxx

Flying has always come easy to me. What is difficult is focusing on the path ahead instead of the thick thighs wrapped around my waist, thighs that belong to the woman who haunts my dreams. With her head pressed to my chest, and her arms locked around my neck, I must restrain myself from giving in to temptation. Especially after last night, when I was seconds away from making her mine.

Her sweet lilac scent overwhelms my senses, gripping her hips tighter, and my cock twitches within the fabric of my breeches.

"You okay, Dragonboy?" she teases, lifting her head to look at me. The loose strands of auburn hair dance around her beautiful face, tempting me to reach out and tuck them back in.

"The question is, are you okay?" I ask her with a smirk, knowing exactly what I plan to do next. Tucking my wings in, I spin us around in a circle and spiral through the clouds.

Her thighs squeeze, her sex grinding into my hardening cock.

"For the love of the gods," I groan. When I straighten again, I hear a laugh leave her and with our bodies pressed together, I can feel it vibrate through me, making me smile.

"Do it again," she said. Tucking my wings in, I swirl again, expecting the clenching of her hips, but she does not do it. She does something even more reckless.

She lets go of me completely. The only thing stopping her from falling to her death is my grip on her hips.

I watch in awe as she spreads her arms wide, leans her head back, and relaxes her legs. An enormous smile spreads across her face while my heart thunders with the adrenaline of this fatal situation.

"What are you doing?" I ask while trying to hook my leg around one of hers.

"Flying."

"You're being reckless," I say.

She lifts her head to look at me. She offers a stern look, but there's a haze in her eyes. "What is the matter, Dragonboy? Afraid I'm going to slip?" She laughs, and I laugh with her until suddenly, her body is no longer in my hands. Panic rises in me as I realize she's slipped from my grip, the sweat and moisture in the air making it impossible to hold on.

I shoot down, my ears trying to tune into a scream, my eyes searching desperately for her. A distant figure below me points me in the right direction.

"Princess," I shout as I fly faster. She cannot die. She will not. I will not fail her. Reaching her, I can see she is still in the same position as before. Her back was to the ground, eyes closed, arms spread wide. Reaching out, I catch her in my arms just before we hit the sea.

An oncoming wave splashes us in its wake as I take off again.

"Open your eyes," I pleaded. Praying her heart did

not give out. "Damnit, Princess, open your eyes."

"Easy, can't a girl get some shut-eye?" she asks, while popping one eye open, as if she did not almost fall to her death.

"Are you serious right now?" I ask her, stopping mid-air, to allow myself to catch my breath and ease the panic.

"Yeah," she scoffs. "Get moving, Dragonboy. Emnera will want us to arrive right behind her."

"I don't take orders from you," I snarl, anger replacing the panic. Not sure if I was angrier at her, not seeming to care about meeting the god of death. Or that I dropped her. Let her slip right through my fingers while she entrusted herself to me.

"Who do you take orders from?"

Her question surprises me. "No one," I answer, while moving forward again.

She shrugs her shoulders, giving me a look of disbelief. "Tell me something," she starts, while burying her face into the crick of my neck.

"What?" My anger melts away as her soft lips graze my neck, sending all the blood in my body to my cock.

"Anything." She stares. Her warm breath teases me further. *Stop it, Jaxx. We are not getting aroused with her in our arms. She is not ours and never will be.*

I try to think of something to say, anything to distract me from my desire to kiss her. *Don't think about what she will taste like.*

"Nothing to say?" Those bright blues search for something in me. Something that I know she will never find. Something I buried deep inside myself the day I failed. The day I allowed my heart to love another.

"Our destination is almost within reach." I don't feel any remorse for not disclosing something about myself. I know she wants something real, but that would be too much.

Our journey is quiet the rest of the way. Abby fell asleep for the last hour. Her chest gently rises and falls with ease.

As we land, Emnera has a fire already set ablaze. She looks at us for a moment but says nothing. I know she knows what happened up there. Her emphatic abilities felt my panic from miles away.

My gaze locks onto the peaceful features of Abby's face. I am tempted to wake her with a kiss, but that would not end well for me. Although she would be worth it, wouldn't she? Leaning down, my lips graze over hers ever so slightly.

"That's not the way to earn a kiss," she murmurs, surprising me again as the tip of her blade presses against my neck.

"You are a sneaky little thing, Princess," I tease against her lips. "Tell me what to do to earn a kiss from your sinful lips."

I see the curiosity in her eyes, feel her pulse quicken with the thought of it. When her body pushes forward, she moves at the last second to whisper in my ear, "Nothing. Your lips will never touch my body." Anger surges through me at her rejecting me. I drop her to the ground, which she hits with a grunt.

"That is not what you were thinking last night. You made the first move, Wildcat. I am just letting you know what could be yours."

"Asshole." She throws her dagger, but I catch it at the last second.

"That is the last time you reject me, Princess. Your last chance to know the pleasure I could bring you with just the touch of my lips. And when you come to your senses and realize that, don't expect me to be waiting for you like some virgin who never got the taste of a woman."

I don't wait for a response; I leave her in the dirt and take my place by the fire.

Calian will arrive soon, and we will breach the castle below us. Then I will exact my vengeance and rid the world of the shadows for the last time.

Chapter Eight

Jaxx

Adorned in all black, I glamorize my wings so they will not be noticeable as Abby and I approach the bottom of the range south of the palace.

Using the cover of nightfall to aid in our camouflage, I tune into the surrounding sounds. I make sure there's no ambush or sentry lying in wait. The surrounding air is silent except for the whispering cool mist coming from the snow-capped mountains from above.

"Well? Doth thou dragon eyes see anything?" she asks in a mocking tone. I feel the corner of my lips quirk up, but she can't see it beneath the cloth we have draped across our faces. When we were plotting this heist, I suggested we dress as those a part of my now non-existent crew. We dressed in all black, including face coverings, to ensure that only our eyes were visible.

The palace looks impregnable from the outside with its steel plated walls, high sentry towers, and iron bars attached to all the windows and gates. Iron would weaken me, but we will not be using any windows or gates to get in.

"Just ahead of us, I can sense the magical door that the eunuch prince told us about," I whisper back, watching for any sign of a patrol.

"Where?" she asks, craning her neck and squinting her eyes.

"Only my dragon eyes can see it," I tease. I catch an eye roll from my peripheral that only makes me want to laugh, but I swallow that down. We wait a few more heartbeats before moving across the soft ground. This earth is soft and made of sand, which helps aid in the quiet nature of our approach.

Moving quickly, we stop behind the low brick outer wall before moving forward to the vacant area directly in front of our target entrance. I feel the humming of magic and taste the ash in my mouth the closer we get to the hidden door.

"Stop," I growl before she triggers the sensor. Her eyes widen at the intensity of my tone. "Don't move until I can disarm the trip wire." She nods in acknowledgment.

Taking another step forward, I call upon my inner dragon, making fire form like gloves in my hands. Unfortunately, the actual black gloves cannot withstand the fire and it incinerates them.

Opening my eyes, I place my palms on the wire that is holding the magic in place, praying to the gods that this will work. Sweat trickles down my brow as I fight to overpower the essence surrounding this wall.

"Jaxx," Abby whispers, but I don't stop. "Hurry. Someone is coming." I cannot hear anything over the increased pulse pounding in my ears.

"One more minute," I hiss while pushing more magic onto the tether until it finally breaks with a loud crack. Knocking me right into the princess. As we tumble, my wings unfurl to cover her so I can take the brunt of the fall as we hit the brick wall we used moments ago to hide from sight.

"What the fuck was that?" Abby hisses while looking at me.

"I don't know," I answer honestly. "Because as many times as I have stolen from rich noble bastards, none of them could get powerful security measures like that one." She stares at me with questions swirling in her eyes.

Our breath mingles in the cool air as she leans closer to me. A noise breaks our eye contact and I at once glamorize my wings again and Abby moves off me so we can squat down and get a visual on the situation.

Two guards in shimmering gilded armor approach with their swords drawn. "If we move now, we can make it inside before they notice it's open and I can glamor the wall again."

"You can really do that?"

"I have many talents, Princess," I smugly say. Before I could decide, the wicked little thing was already half-way to the secret entrance, her long braided hair waving at me from behind. Running, I quickly catch up to her just as she enters through the hollowed-out hole.

Panting, she raises her hands above her head to allow more air to push into her lungs while I am barely winded. Moving toward her, she backs up into the brick wall behind her as I pin her with my hips.

"What are you—"

I place my right hand over her mouth and bring a finger over mine, motioning for silence. She nods in understanding, so I remove my hand, but the rest of me feels fused to the floor beneath us. With her body pressed against mine again, a flood of inappropriate thoughts rushes straight to my cock.

From the corner of my eye, I see the two guards silently signaling to each other that no one is here. Both appear oblivious to the fact that a secret entrance should be right where Abby and I are standing.

She remains still. Her chest rises and falls with the growing tension of being caught. I can feel the peaks of her breasts pressing through the fabric of her tunic and I know now is not the most opportune time, but I have had enough waiting.

Without thinking, I catch her chin with my hand, tilting her head to the perfect angle, pull the fabric from around her mouth and mine, then push my lips against hers. It is soft. One might not count it as a kiss, but then I press deeper, savoring the stolen moment.

I pull back ever so slightly to see if she will return a kiss. Her lips found my mine and soon her hands wrap around my neck, pulling me into her. My tongue pierces through hers as I hoist her hips into the air. My lips find the soft skin right below her ear and a moan releases her.

"Jaxx," she breathlessly says.

"Princess."

"Now is not the time," she says and I pull back, letting her feet touch the ground before clearing my throat and stepping away from her.

"The dagger, right?" I turn away from her, reaching down to adjust myself before turning to look down the corridor. It's pitch black, so I spark a small fireball in my hand to light the way.

The air is silent with unspoken words, and I feel

like a fool for kissing her. Especially on an important mission such as this. My focus needs to be on avenging my family, not some woman. Even a woman as fucking perfect as her.

"So," she starts. I don't look at her, but keep moving forward down this never-ending tunnel. "You want to talk about it?"

"Talk about what?"

"What happened back there?" she said. I remain silent, worried I'd sound like a fool. Her hand grips my arm, stopping me. "Come on, Dragonboy, don't tell me you're unable to speak."

I grip her shoulders and pin her to the wall again. "I'm hunting for the most important relic ever known—wasting time talking about some pathetic, foolish mistake means nothing to me. I don't give a fuck. I have kissed plenty of women, and now I kissed a shrewd princess—twice. Sorry to tell you this, sweetheart, but you're not special."

It was cruel, and every bit tasted like acid on my tongue. But it needed to be said. What I feel is not important. The mission is, and if I need to make her hate me so she does not get hurt, then so be it.

"Get the fuck away from me," she growls. I can hear the anger in her tone but see the hurt in her eyes. I, at once, want to apologize, but I just bite my cheek and move away from her. "There is nothing special about you either, Jaxx."

Abby pushes past me. Coldness washes over me, replacing the warmth I felt when her body pressed against mine.

After walking for another hour, we stop to look around. Nothing but walls in front and to the sides of us. The entrance we came through is nothing but a distant glimmer. "Something isn't right," Abby states.

Looking around, I try to pinpoint any magic, but I sense nothing. "We need to get out of here."

"Why?" she asks.

"Because, Princess, I feel nothing."

"What do you mean?"

"I mean," I say, turning toward her. "There is no magic in here."

"Still not seeing the point."

"The point is, Princess, is that I feel nothing. Which means something is blocking me. Blocking my magic. And there is only one thing that can do that."

"Iron. It surrounded us," she finally says as the revelation crosses her face. Before we could move any further, the floor beneath us dissipates and I fall into darkness. The faint scream of Abby pushes through my mind as I reach out for her. My wings burst from my back as I fight to keep us from crashing. Pulling her body flush with mine, I zoom in to see how far the drop will be, when I feel the floor under my feet again. The rushing in my ears and panic in my chest are gone.

Looking around, I can see it. Sitting on a velvet bed of gold, encased in a transparent glass case, is the weapon that is going to kill the Dark Wizard finally.

"This doesn't feel right," Abby states, but my eyes only stay on the dagger. Glinting off the soft glow from the fire in my palm is a dagger of pure gold. From the hilt, along the jagged edges, to the end that will soon be coated with my enemy's blood.

Taking a step forward, I reach out with my magic, trying to sense any presence of a trap, but again, I feel nothing. Not even my magic is working.

"Jaxx..." I hear Abby yell my name, but it's already too late. Heat burns through me, and I taste metallic dust coating my tongue as I fall forward. "What's wrong?" Abby asks and I try to speak, but my throat is closing up. "Jaxx, tell me what's happening." Somehow, I end up in her arms. I see the panic in her eyes, hear the rapid beat of her heart, and feel the warmth of her body.

Reaching up to her, I touch her face because if I am going to die, then I want to feel her. Not the stone-cold surface of this death trap. Her head swings from side to side. Looking for the explanation I cannot seem to give her. Swallowing hard, I croak out two words.

"Iron. Dagger."

She looks confused at first, but as my eyes begin to close and death clouds my vision, I see the faintest image of an auburn-haired woman grabbing a golden blade and fighting off a circle of five guards. A familiar lilac scent consumes me, washing away the lingering taste of metal as darkness consumes me.

Chapter Nine

Abbygale

Guards surround us, and the one person who has magic is unconscious. "Well, who wants to die first?" The guards surrounding me snicker. They all come at once. I duck a blow to mean for my head while blocking the strike at my knees. I swipe my leg out and knock two on their backs while flipping backwards out of the way of two clashing swords. My back hits the wall to the right with a crunch, and I see stars for a few seconds before jumping to my feet.

I raise the gilded blade, ready for the last three guards. "Three against one. The odds are not in your favor."

They exchange a look with one another. Clearly, my bluff is not working. I bend down, gripping the extra dagger in my left boot and before the middle guard knew what hit him, my blade was sticky with his blood. "Three down, two to go. Are you certain you don't want to turn tail and run?"

"Oh, I don't think they should be the ones who back down." Weakness and fatigue wash over me and I fall to the floor with a thud. I try to form words, but even my tongue is swelling. "Don't fight it, little princess. It'll only make it worse."

When I awaken, a rope is around my neck, and I

can hear Emnera arguing with the men who captured us. When I look over to my side, I see Jaxx hanging next to me. I see Calian and Emnera fighting, but Cal looks weakened. I gasp when he falls to his enemies, blood coating the solid surface of the courtyard. Glancing in Jaxx's direction, I see him. His face is hardened, and his shoulders are back. His wings try to flex, but they cannot seem to find the strength. I am not sure what to do or say. I can hear Emnera's screams of pain and anguish piercing the air just before her light cuts through the ropes.

Jaxx helps me to my feet. "Jaxx," he holds up a hand to stop me. I look toward my new friend. My heart aches as she cradles her dead mate in her arms. My eyes become misty, but instead of letting the sorrow I feel at another loss, I buck up and head inside to find the chest. Jaxx is quick to follow.

Chapter Ten

Jaxx

Our walk through the narrow corridors was silent, not even the sound of a rat or mouse scurrying about. It was almost deafening. I did not realize my brother and Abby were so close. The pain and grief she is feeling over his loss is astounding. Would she react the same way about me? Not that I should care. We are not even friends. Sharing two kisses does not mean I automatically fall head over heels for her. What am I talking about? I just watched my baby brother get killed. Why am I not more upset about this?

It is the gut wrenching feeling—I just know he isn't dead. I don't know how, but something deep inside tells me he's not really gone. Could it be false hope or denial? Maybe.

"You know that silent conversation in your head would be of use if it could actually talk back to you." Abby's croaked voice broke through the silence.

"Not sure you'd enjoy a sneak peek inside my head," I teased, and she stopped dead in her tracks. I stopped with her and took in the sorrow filled features of her face. Her deep blue eyes shimmer like twin deep pools of water ready to overflow. Dirt clings to her tear-soaked cheeks and her lips tremble as she tries to hold back emotions.

Growling, she steps up to me. "Your brother is dead, and you think it's appropriate to joke?" she growls, questioning me rather than asking. I was expecting a punch or a slap, but she just shook her head in disappointment. "Emnera is right not to trust you. An emotionless asshole who does not care about anyone or anything except himself and his goals."

The audacity of this woman to stand here and insult me. Curling my fingers into fists, I resist the urge to pin her to the wall and teach her a lesson on manners.

"If you are assuming I didn't care for my baby brother, then you are sadly mistaken." I keep my growing temper in check.

"Well, you could have fooled me. You are a criminal, a liar, and a thief. Let us not forget about the murderer." The hate in her eyes hits me like a thousand knives.

"I guess you've decided about me, then?" My nostrils flare so quickly I am surprised to see smoke spewing out from them.

"Yeah. Not like you would care what I think." She turns to walk away. Gripping her shoulders, I pull her flush against me. Her back hits my chest as I lock her arms to her sides and whisper in her ear, "The thing about me, Princess, is I know what happens to you when it's just us." I bait her while pressing my lips to her neck and smiling as she tilts it further to give me more access. "Your heart rate quickens, your pussy throbs, and you ache for my touch. That is why you kissed me. That is why you want to fight with me. To give you a reason to hate me."

"I hate you," she growls. But her body betrays her words. "I wish it were you and not Cal."

The venom in her words makes me instantly let go. She steps away and continues to move down the winding corridors. When I catch up to her, we are standing in front of a large double steel door with iron handles.

"Abby," I said, but she hushed me. I don't know why I want to reconcile with her. Want to know if that is truly what she feels for me. But as I step up to take her hand, she moves forward and opens the doors.

The scent of leather and ale fills my nose as we walk onto a plush satin rug. Everything is gold plated and black. Common theme for this kingdom, but we don't stop to look at everything. We search for the dagger.

Overturning the cushions upon the settee, flipping through the enlarged mattress and silk-covered pillows, I growl in frustration. "Where the fuck is it?"

"Calm down, Dragonboy." Abby's tone is different. It went from hate to playful in the blink of an eye. I narrowed my eyes at her suspiciously. "Come over here."

She points to the spot directly beside her. I don't see it until I am right next to her. Sitting in a crafted hole under the hard floor is a golden chest big enough to hold the dagger. We kneel, my fingers tingling with the anticipation of holding it.

Together, we lift the chest from the hole and place it between us. There is joy in her eyes again, and I cannot help but smile. We direct our attention to the chest in front of us and try to open it, but it's sealed. It is only then I taste it.

"It's magically sealed," I tell her as I feel the ash coating my tongue.

"I guess we need his blood for this, too," she says with a shrug. That brief second of joy fades and I don't know whether it was what she said. Or that I needed to prove something to her or myself. But I reached over, cupping her face, and claimed her lips.

I was afraid she would pull away or threaten to stab me like before, but she fell into my arms, gripping the back of my neck to pull me on top of her. I wedged myself between her thighs while deepening our kiss. My tongue piercing through hers, a moan escapes her, and went straight to my cock.

I broke our kiss, but placed my forehead against hers. "I loved my baby brother. Although he did not know it, I have watched over him since the day I gave him to that woman."

"I didn't mean it," she says, and I immediately recognize the subject of her comment. "My wish is for you not to die. I hope no one dies. I cannot..." She pauses, and I hush her with a gentle kiss.

"Well, well, looks like we just walked in on the good part," a husky male voice said from the threshold of the door. We were instantly on our feet. I put myself in front of Abby and the chest. Knowing she could take care of herself, but not wanting anything to happen to her. My wings burst from my back as two blades of fire form from my hands.

"Sorry about the cock-block, boy, but we came here for two things." The man had yellow teeth, and a red bandanna wrapped around his bald head. Two others accompanied him, also wearing a red bandanna around their heads. I could have sworn I saw a Griffin imprinted on the front.

"Red Griffin Bandits," Abby mutters as she

searches for some type of weapon. When the guards drag us from the secret corridor, they took all our weapons, to include her daggers.

"You know these men?" I ask her.

"They were criminals back in Orion. I thought the last one died during the war we had with Emperor Santana," she replied.

"What's that, Princess?" the bald man asks. "You thought we were all slaughtered?" He feigned a laugh, pulling out a dagger. "No, you see, when I got word that two women killed my sons, I thought, there is no fucking way. But when I got word that they were the Princesses of Orion who did it, then I thought that is impossible." His cold blue eyes darken and narrow on her. Something possessive comes out of me.

"Easy, freak. I will not hurt her yet." Spit came from his mouth as he enunciated his last syllable. "You give over the girl and the chest, and you can go free."

This pathetic human thinks he can bargain with me? I charge at him, but he knocks me down when he connects two large iron chains to my torso. The breath seized in my lungs as I hit the back wall. Memories of my failure flooded my mind again. The night my parents died, I was too weak.

Through flooded vision, I see her fighting them. Just like before, only this time, I call upon my fire. Upon the dragon that stays dormant. With a loud roar, my canines sharpen, my fingernails form into talons, and fire pushes its way to the surface.

"Run," I yell to Abby, and she grabs the chest and takes off while the three bandits are stunned in place. Before Abby could make it too far, the bald man holds a dagger to her throat.

"I will kill her if you attack," he threatens.

Without hesitation, I throw my fire toward them. Abby moves at the last possible second before my fire hits its targets, incinerating them. As I run toward her, I notice that I didn't completely miss her—her right shoulder has blisters and burns.

"I'm sorry. I didn't mean to harm you." I want to touch her, but my heart beat is only increasing. "I don't know how to turn it off."

Wincing, she sits up and reaches out to me, but I jerk back. "It's okay. Just trust me."

I look into her eyes as my heart rate slows. She raises her un-injured hand to my face, and I instantly feel her presence taming the beast inside me. A connection that is becoming stronger each time I am near her.

"It is okay, Jaxx. I am okay."

"Do you trust *me*?" I ask, and she nods. Placing my right hand on her injured shoulder, she winces at first, but I focus on the burn. Focus on how I want to take the pain away. The pain I caused her, and consume it. There is heat at first, but then nothing. I feel her soft skin under my palm again.

"You healed me," she whispers in awe.

"I just focused like I did with Ziran," I admit, shrugging like it was no big deal. Abby cups my face and then sticks a finger in my mouth to examine my teeth. "They are back to normal."

"Good," she says. But when she pulls me in for another kiss, I have to fight the urge to take her right here, right now.

"We need to go," I say and she sighs in defeat. We stand, and I grab the case and then her. Both cradled in my arms, I flex my wings. "Ready, Princess?"

She winks at me, and I take off down the hall using my wings. I'm so lost in thoughts about what just happened that I barely register how wide and tall my wings are.

As I look at the blue-eyed woman in my arms, something sparks inside me. The walls around my heart burst into a million pieces as the realization strikes.

My mate.

Part Two: Within in the walls of Immorteum

Chapter Eleven

Jaxx

I am dead inside, and I love it. I no longer have the emotions of humanity stopping me from stabbing a hole through Rai's chest.

After I took off with Shadow Killer, I found a nice hiding spot to bury the trove that holds my pathetic heart inside. Not that anyone could break the blood magic. After scoping out the Jian desert, I found the route Rai's men take to and from the hidden fortress. Upon flying back toward the Great Sea, I observed the Petunia was moored up.

My eyes caught sight of her. The woman with the long brown hair. Her lilac scent haunts me every day. I know I used to feel something for her when my heart was beating in my chest, but not any longer. She means nothing to me.

"Master has ordered the entire regiment to attack the realm in full force," one scout tells another. They cannot see me hidden behind two large boulders.

"We are to attack without warning and to kill anyone who doesn't submit," the other states.

Shadow Killer buzzes with the anticipation of killing.

"Not yet." I speak as if the object can hear me. "You are destined for one man and one man only, but it is not the right moment yet."

As the scouts disappear beyond the magic barrier, I stay out until the White Sun is making its rise. The next patrol will come through, and that will be my moment to strike.

A few heartbeats later, two soldiers walk through the barrier and I pounce. Slitting their throats and coating my hands in their warm crimson fluids, I drag their bodies to the other side of the barrier before covering up the blood path in the sand.

Approaching the invisible wall, I place my hands on it, praying to the gods it works, and push through.

On the other side, a large black tower with an attached arena stares back at me.

There are no patrols, which seems odd, but to a smug bastard like Rai, it is no issue. Fatal mistake on his part. I run to the wall and scale it, using my wings to ascend covertly to the highest point.

I make it to a window seal and take a quick glance, noticing a figure sleeping on a bed. Stupid bastard.

I silently jiggle with the lock, and it opens with ease. Slipping inside, I notice the room is barren except for one bed, two shelves of jarred heads, and a small writing table.

I don't have time to rummage through the papers as I raise the Shadow Killer and mutter the last words he will ever hear.

"And now you die, and justice is served." The blade pierces through cloth and skin as blood pulls. I step back and look at my triumph, trying to feel something. Anything for what I just did, but I feel nothing.

A clapping noise comes from behind me. I turn

around and see him.

"No!" I growl.

"I will give you credit for your effort, but other than that, you failed," he says as I reach for Shadow Killer, but it vanishes along with the body. "Did you honestly believe you could sneak into my palace and kill me?"

"I killed you."

"No, you killed an illusion of me. Nice blade," he mocks, swinging the golden dagger from hand to hand.

"You will die for your sins," I snarl.

"I don't see why everyone hates me so much. I was just trying to bring their kingdom to its knees under one monarch. Is that so bad?"

"By killing innocents."

"You think your parents were innocent? Foolish boy." I take a step forward. His immediate reaction was to point Shadow Killer's tip at me. "Down, boy. Would not want this to impale you."

"Give it to me and it won't," I say.

He stares at me, insulting me further. "I really ought to thank you for bringing this to me. I wonder, though, how you broke the blood seal?" He is fishing for answers, but something tells me he already knows. "Oh, right, you gave up your heart. How honorable." He feigns admiration. "I don't want to kill you, Jaxx. I would like to offer you a deal."

"No." I spit at his feet.

"Now don't be too hasty. I promise it will be just as delicious for you, too."

"You take whatever you're offering and shove it up your ass," I growl. My wings are flexing and ready to strike.

"I mean, I was going to offer you the safety of your woman, but…" he trails off, baiting me.

"I don't have a woman," I spit out.

"Oh, okay." He snaps his fingers. The lilac scent hits me before my eyes lock onto hers.

"I don't know what makes you think she is mine." If I had a heart, I am sure it would beat for this girl.

"Would you care if I hurt her?" he asks, and I do, but not because she is mine, but because she is an innocent woman.

"I won't let you hurt an innocent."

"So, you are telling me you don't want harm to come to her because she is innocent? Not because she is your mate?" Abby's blue eyes narrow in confusion. I did not have time to tell her before all this happened.

"Correct."

"All right, well, you can save her if you let me go with the dagger. You two will just get exiled to another realm of my choosing. Doesn't that sound fun?" He jumps up and down like the madman he is.

"No," Abby states for the first time. "I don't want to be anywhere near him."

"Oh, lovers' quarrel. This just got interesting," Rai states as he looks between us.

"We aren't lovers," I say.

"That's for damn sure," Abby agrees. I am confused why she is mad at me and not the man that has taken her prisoner.

"What are you doing here, anyway?" I asked her.

"I was hunting down the traitor that took Shadow Killer and ran off," she says, standing a little taller. I am surprised she found me. "I shou…we should have never trusted a criminal like you. And if he does not kill you after this, I will."

"Yes. Keep going." Rai encourages, and I growl at him.

"Let the woman go. Your fight is with me."

"No, I don't think I will." Blades of fire form in my curled fists. "I think I am going to send you two very far away from here as a punishment for your crimes against me." The guards push Abby into me, and I grip her hips, steadying her.

"Don't touch me," she says, and I let her go.

"If you can survive this new place and make it back before your family dies, then I will be impressed," Rai says. "Otherwise, goodbye. When you see your lost love again, dear Princess, you can send me a thank you prayer."

Before either of us can utter a word, a vortex of black and green swallows us. Taking us from one realm to the next.

When I come to, I'm on a bed of crunchy grass. The sky above me is hollow and there is no light. Getting to my feet, I look around to figure out where we are when I come face to face with a fuming five-foot three brown haired woman.

Her dainty fists connect with my jaw.

"How the fuck did you get out of your cuffs?" She does not answer me as her other fist connects with my other side. Gripping both her wrists, I pin them to the small of her back while turning her.

"Let me go," she growls.

"Easy, Princess. I am not the bad guy here. I just saved your ass."

"No, you idiot. You killed everyone back home. All of them will die because of you."

"I'm sure the others will stop him and if not, I will find us a way back home." Something familiar comes with the contact of her skin against mine. I am not sure what, but it is almost warm.

"Let go of me." She jerks out of my grasp.

"Promise to behave?" I say, and she nods. I let her back away a few feet. Admiring the curves of her body. I may not have a heart, but I still have a cock. She doesn't turn back toward me, only moves forward in hurried steps.

"Where are you going?" I yell, but she says nothing. Instead, she gestures an insult toward me with both of her middle fingers.

As I look around, I try to find an opening for me to take flight, but when I flex my wings, I feel them being weighed down. Immobile. *Fuck.*

I charge after the Princess, catching up with her easily and grip her arm.

"Don't touch me." There is so much hate in her eyes. I only grip her arm tighter.

"Did I offend you?"

She jerks her arm free and I let it go as she scoffs at me. "Are you daft, or did you hit your head on the way here?" I raise a brow at her. "Gods, just leave me alone."

"That is not wise in a place like this."

"Why?" she asks.

"Take a look around you. Everything is dead or dying. There is no sun, and you don't know anyone here. We don't know if someone lives in this place."

"Fine. Just don't touch me. I will not hesitate to stab you–with this branch. The only reason you are still breathing is because I don't have a weapon." She means every word by the adamant stare she's throwing my way.

"Fine, let's just figure out where we are first and how to get back home before you stab me."

She rolls her eyes but agrees.

Chapter Twelve

Abbygale

One year later
"Do you remember the plan, Wildcat?"
I blinked.

Jaxx shrugs his shoulders, not understanding that every new nickname he gives me just makes me want to stab him even more. "Just follow my lead, Dragonboy."

I push forward, but he grips my shoulder, jerking me backward. My daggers are at his neck faster than he can wrap those thick arms around me. His emerald eyes narrow as he leans forward, snarling, "Keep calling me 'boy' and I might just have to show you how much of a man I really am."

A knot forms in my throat at the intensity of his words, but I don't falter. I will never show a weakness for him, or any other man, again. "We have a mission to complete. I, for one, would like to eat something warm for dinner tonight." He does not move, but I press the blades deeper until a bead of blood forms. "Back away. Right now."

I narrow my eyes and step closer to him. The heat radiating from his body warms the cool breeze brushing against my exposed skin. I usually dress from head to toe in all black for these missions. Ever since being trapped in this realm over a year ago, we have done what we could to survive until finally finding a way out. There is a rumor that if we get in good with the one called Scarr, then he will tell us how to get out of this hellhole and back to the surface.

Back to Dalaria.

Jaxx leans forward until a breath of space is between us, inhaling my scent as he always does when moments like this happen. He is on the verge of losing himself completely to the darkness that has replaced his once beating heart. "Easy, Wildcat. Retract your claws, and I will retract mine."

The sharp cut of his blade digs into my navel, and I swallow hard. I know I am bluffing, but with Jaxx; it is hard to tell. I do as he asks, and he backs away before we pull our face mask up to only our eyes showing. Our mission is not the easiest one. Rumors say that where we're going is the deadliest camp in all of Immorteum. Umbra Dolor is a rigid landscape, with the hardened stone as sharp as a needle meant for sewing. They say the smallest brush against one edge feels like the cut of a thousand. Your skin will be beyond repair and death is certain.

Jaxx and I move like the waves of the ocean colliding with the push of the wind. The air is quiet. Which means the slightest nudge of the pea-gravel beneath our feet could give us away. We bend down behind a pointed boulder, peeking out from both sides, and looked into the glowing flames of the camp. Emerald burns bright against the murky backdrop of this place.

"There are about ten outside, but at least another twenty huts. What do you say, break even?" Jaxx whispers from my right.

"No. We get in, grab the artifact, and get out before they catch us."

"You're no fun, Princess."

I ignore him and make the first move, crawling to the next boulder and then on to the next, until I can get a better view of the entire camp. I look up and see the ledge of a twenty-foot hill. Pulling another pair of black gloves over my current ones, I ease up the side. The thicker gloves have added protection and rubber grip on the palms to aid in my advance. My boots have thick rubber heels to protect against the pointed ends of this rock side cutting through.

I ascend the narrow path. Each step and handhold fuels my desire to leave this godforsaken wasteland. Only the dead belong in this place. Not for living souls just passing through. But I did not die. An evil wizard who has destroyed my home pushed me through a portal; Dalaria. I think of my big sister, Kaleigh, and brother-in-law, Rowland. How have they been doing since I have been down here? Is she looking for me? The one thing my sister is good at is, aside from her archery skills, is finding what she is looking for. I imagine with the power of the dragons on her side, she could bring me home.

My hand slips and the surface at my toes buckle, causing me to lose my balance. My right arm burns with the weight of my body as I hang off the edge. I hiss in pain as my stomach rubs the side of the hill. "Fuck!" I whisper-yell.

Something warm coats my shirt, and as I look down, I notice a tear in my shirt and that someone has cut my stomach's skin. A warm hand covers it, sending flames of green while I fall. Another arm wraps around me and the free hand covers my cries. Warm lips caress my ear with calming whispers, "Easy, Wildcat. I've got you. Let the pain heal you." My visions flickers in and out, and when I come to, I find myself on the ground outside of a vast tent.

I sit up, holding my aching side. I look to see a small pink scar formed over it and then search for him. Jaxx is kneeling, looking around, seeming to find a way inside. I crawl to his side.

"Have a nice nap, Wildcat."

"Remind me to thank you after we escape," I whisper. Jaxx smirks and then goes back to scanning the area ahead of us. "Is this the leader's tent? Soto said the artifacts were inside."

"I am not sure, but unless we snatch someone and ask them, we will be here until sunrise searching. All the tents have a uniform appearance. There is no way to tell. A smart strategy, if you ask me." He pulls out a dagger. "I'll cut a little hole for us to peek inside."

I grip his wrist before the tip touches the fabric. "You can snag only one. But be careful, Jaxx. They are called the Bloodscars for a reason."

"For a moment there, I thought you actually cared about me." He leans in closer to say, "You getting soft on me, Wildcat?"

I smirk before closing the distance ever so slightly. "Never." He looks down to where the tip of my dagger sits right at his cock.

A slight growl rumbles in his throat before his hand snatches my chin, and he pulls me in, placing a chaste kiss on my lips. "One more chance, Wildcat. Either make your move, or I will."

He lets go of me and is gone before I can

understand what just happened. It was the first time his lips brushed against mine in over a year. My heart cinches at the memories of what used to be. Of what could have been before he made that stupid deal that took everything away from us. I feel my eyes misting over, but I shake it out of my head and pull myself together. "He chose glory over you, and he would do it again."

At that moment, I mentally agreed to keep my distance from him. No more teasing glances or brushes of the skin. No more, because one thing is for damned sure—Jaxx will not keep me from getting back home and killing Rai.

"I am done playing this mind game with you, Jaxx. You screwed up when you scaled your heart in that chest. How about we focus on the true mission here?"

His emerald gaze connects with mine and I wait on bated breath for him to move. To speak. "We have been here a year, Princess. Not sure why you are in a rush now."

I scoff, shaking my head from side to side. "We would have been gone sooner if you had not been whoring your way through every creature within a short distance from us. While you have been wetting your wick, I have been building a re-pour with every mercenary here, and I believe we are closer to getting back to Dalaria. Now, come down from your high horse and help me secure one of these bastards so we can find that damn artifact."

Jaxx's smirk goes into a thin line, his eyes ever scrutinizing before backing away gracefully. "Very well, Princess. Give me a sec."

As he slips into the shadows, I secure my dagger,

waiting for him to return. It was a mere minute, I believe, before a body thudded in front of me. A gag secured around his mouth while his hands remained bound. Scars littered the exposed skin of his forearms, almost reminding me of pink flames dancing along his skin.

I lean down while Jaxx jerks his head back so I can meet his eyes. I lean down at the prisoner. "Tell me where I can find the artifact. Scream, and I'll slit your throat," I threaten and he nods.

Jaxx lowers the gag but places his blade against the man's Adam'sapple. "If you mean the ash crown, it's secured in bogs where all the tortured and trapped souls reign," the prisoner answers.

"I see." I look at Jaxx.

"How do we know you're telling the truth?" Jaxx asks.

The prisoner shrugs his shoulders. "Kill me, let me go. It doesn't matter because you will not survive the journey. No one has ever retrieved the ashen crown from where it slumbers. Many have tried, and all have died. Why do you think the price is so high on it? Every mercenary lord wants it."

"Why?" I pressed.

"The one who wears the crown will have access to its primordial power. Giving them the ability to jump realms. Manipulate time and space."

A part of me believes him. The other, it is the wall that protects me from trusting too easily.

Jaxx looks at me, then nods. "Which god has blessed this crown?" The prisoner's brow rises in silent questioning.

By the wrinkle in his brow, he was thinking about

it. "One would have to be the god of time, and the others goddess of some sort. According to the legend, when the realms were created, each primordial was given life upon them. Creating any and everything within it. Each ruler received an artifact that granted them the power of the primordial. Humans had the dragons. Immorteum had the ashen crown. And any other realm had either wizards, witches, relics of unknown power. I can't believe you two don't know this. I thought every child in this realm knew the stories?"

I smiled, then got closer to him. "We're not from around here. Now, can this crown allow its wielder the ability to jump realms?"

He shook his head up and down. "I can only assume. That would be the reason my commander wants it."

"And any other lord down here?" Jaxx added.

"If they can jump realms, there is no telling whose side they would be on. We need to get that crown before anyone else," I tell him.

"What should we do with him?" Jaxx asks.

I look at the prisoner. "What skills do you have?"

"Skills?" he asks.

I sigh. "Can you hunt? Cook?"

"Oh, well, I can sing."

"Great. He can sing our enemies to death. I'll kill him." Jaxx presses the blade deep across his neck and I watch as the rich scarlet color of blood slowly drips from the wound. It wouldn't take long for him to die.

When I meet Jaxx's gaze again, his eyes are alight with green fire. The hairs on the back of my neck stand as I remain ensnared in his gaze, repeating my mantra

over and over in my head.
I will not falter.
I will not fail.

Chapter Thirteen

Jaxx

I wipe my blade clean with a spare cloth as Abby stares me down. She does this every time I kill in front of her, and it makes me eager to peek inside of her head. Our little game of chase is getting old. If I wanted to, not a soul in this realm would turn me away—but despite what she thinks, I've kept my wick dry, and this little princess will not turn me away for much longer.

My heart sits in a chest in the hands of our common enemy back in Dalaria. Not sure if I care to retrieve the organ. Having a heart seems like too much trouble than it's worth.

"We could've used him." She breaks the silence finally.

I smirk. "We just did."

"You know, I meant to lead us through the damn bogs. Flumen Immortuorum is the river of souls and impossible to survive, let alone swim in to retrieve the ashen crown," Abby answers, bending over the dead man's body, patting him down for anything.

I disregard the rumored dangers of this fucking bog and respond, "Immortality at its best. No heart, Princess."

Abby finishes her search of the bastard before walking up to me. Her lilac scent will never get old. It's embedded in her skin, just as it is in my memories of us when I had my heart. Every time she pops into my thoughts, the memory of her lips pressed to mine, skin against my own, the feelings void of emotion. It was as if I was just going through the motions with her.

"Jaxx, you may be unkillable now, but your soul is still inside of you. They reap souls in this bog. That's how it stays functional as a barrier between the lands. Our side and the other side, protecting its mysteries from all the warlords and mercenaries over on this side. If they take your soul, there will be nothing but a shell in there. Is that what you want?" Her blue eyes soften for a moment.

I flip my dagger in my hand twice until the hilt is back in my grip, and then press the cool steel against her cheek. A red blush appears instantly. Usually, she has her daggers ready, but not this time. I lean in close until they were a mere breath from one another. The minted paste she used this morning was still fresh against my nose. "Are you worried that if I lose my soul, I will be a shell? Or are you worried that you'll never be able to restore my heart?" I wait for her to falter. But she never does, and that's the interesting fact about this human woman. "What is your true reason for wanting to leave this realm?"

When she doesn't answer, I take her silence as her response and back away, tucking my dagger back into its sleeve. Abby adverts her gaze from mine before spinning on her heel and walks back toward the exit. The territory known as Silva Mortis is on the other side of this godforsaken rock death trap. There isn't much to it, but the people that live here, dead or alive, have made it in a livable city. As you cross the ridgeline over

Umbra Dolor, you enter a forest of withered branches. There are no trees. Just tall, dead trunks with sharp sticks poking out. Everything about this realm is torturous.

Finding comfort in a place of such mystery is baffling to me. But Sotto's City has made a vast effort. When Abbygale and I first arrived in this realm, I wasn't sure how we would survive without my full powers. The realm restricts my ability to take flight and use my other skills. The guards outside the city greet us as we approach. I must bite the inside of my cheek as they put their hands on her. Everyone gets patted down for weapons. You can own them, you just need to turn them in to the city and watch at the gate before entering the city.

This is Lord Sottos' way of supporting peace within the community. When I come behind Abby, she has that beautiful smile plastered across her face. The young guard in conversation with her is absolutely stricken with her beauty. My ears twitch as I listen in on their conversation. "There is nothing across the border except death and deserters," the guard reminds her.

"I just needed to see for myself," she responds.

"Adventuring out past the city is not for young woman as pretty as you." He gives her a smirk. Although you cannot see anything past the half-face mask he wears, I can see it in his green eyes. "There are many dangers beyond the walls."

I cross my arms over my chest, watching with amusement as Abby clenches her hands into fists at her sides. They have not taken her hidden dagger tucked deep in her right boot. She takes a step closer to the man. "And do you think that just because I'm a woman,

I cannot protect myself?"

He eyes her from head to toe and says, "I'm just saying that you need protection. Women are not meant to fight."

Idiot.

This time, I move because I've seen this before. I ensnare her arm in a vise grip and push past the guard. "We are leaving. Thank you, guard, for your encouraging words."

Abbygale struggles in my grip, jerking and scratching my leathers. "Let me go, Jaxx."

"Not until you calm down. I don't want to spend another night in the cells, do you?" I whisper in her ear.

We make it past the entrance, but I hold on to her, dragging her past the marketplace crowd. Several vendors yell at us about their homemade foods and crafts. There would be no time for shopping right now. I have tunnel vision. Keeping one goal in mind. Get home before she makes a fool of herself. After making it through the market, we pass several buildings that people use for homes. Our building is farthest away from everyone.

It's a small shack with only one bedroom, fireplace, and bathing chamber. I open the door, throw her inside, and then slam the front door, placing the bolt to secure the entrance before spinning around to face her. Just as I expected, she charges me, her small fist flying, but I catch her wrist, spinning us and pinning her to the wall. I thrust my knee between her legs, grip both her wrists in my left hand, then wrap a gentle hand around her neck, snarling. "Calm down, Wildcat."

"You have no right to manhandle me like that." Her eyes alight with rage, reminding me of a blue dragon fire. "I can handle myself in front of misogynistic men."

"So, you weren't going for your secret dagger and go all stabby on him?"

She refutes my statement. Her mouth moves up and down, but remains silent before looking away in shame. I don't like that.

My hand moves on its own from her neck to her chin and I force her to look at me. "If you want to stab every fucker in this place that degrades you just because you were born a female, Princess, do it. Hell, I'll help you and be your number one fucking fan while doing it. But there is a time and a place for such actions. And if you ever want to see your family again, you need to control that anger you have. Find another outlet."

"I'm not angry. I'm furious."

"Good. Now use that as your motivation to help find the damn ashen crown so we can get the fuck out of this place. What do you say?" I slowly back away from her. Abby stares at me and in that moment I see her fire simmer just a smidge.

"If you ever put your hands on me like that again, you won't have to worry about me losing control anymore." Her threat didn't scare me, but it did something else entirely. A feeling deep within me rose and I'm not sure what it was, so I buried it back down. "I'm getting that crown. Even if I must die trying."

"Don't worry about that, Wildcat. I'll make sure if you die, your sister knows you died a fool," I warn her because the look she is giving me tells me she is going to go after it without preparation. "We need to get into the damn bogs without our souls being yanked. You need to clear your head, Princess. Go take a nap. Drink water or eat something. Anything to get whatever stick is up your ass, *out*."

Abby's nose visibly wrinkles. "I need to hit something. I'm out of practice."

"You want to hit something? Then hit me. Fight me." I offer my jaw. "Go ahead. I know you want to." I tease just a little.

"You want to fight me?" she asks, and I wasn't sure if she was seeking clarification or permission. I nodded.

"I'll be your punching bag all day, every day, if it prevents you from going into the stockades." It felt like the most sincere thing I've said in the past year.

"Why do you care what happens to me?" It comes out as a whisper and her eyes simmer just a little more. She visibly relaxes a little more, and a crack is forming inside of her. A wall she built around herself when I broke our bond that never was. I clear my throat and then release her chin from my grip, creating a space between us before turning my back to her and flexing my shoulders. I look over my shoulder at her before speaking.

"You're my ticket out of here, Princess. You're the price I'm willing to pay for revenge."

Chapter Fourteen

Abbygale

Jaxx spent the rest of the evening into the next morning out of the house. I was grateful for the time apart. Cinnamon yeast wafted into my room, making my empty stomach arouse me from my sleep. Not that I've been able to get a goodnight rest since I watched my boyfriend get killed by a shadow beast two years ago. I still can see his face sometimes when I close my eyes. The deceitfulness of the creature that took control of his soul to the last second when it killed him from the inside out. He had no fear. No regret. And I often wonder if he was in pain when it happened?

A heavy sigh escaped me as I laced my boots up. Tucking my small dagger into my boot and ensuring the long leather skirt covers. I pulled on my black tank and walked out of the room. Appreciating the smallness of it. Only one bed and a single drawer were in it. There wasn't even a window to admire the starless sky. The two foot walk to the conjoining main room only had a two-seat settee. Jaxx always folded his small blanket and cushion neatly at the right end. Toward the back of the house, just a few strides away, was the trove where we could cook our meals over a small fire pit.

When I entered, my mouth watered the second my eyes landed on his exposed broad back. Jaxx was shirtless. I could see his back that mapped out the battle wounds of his youth. Judging by the tiny droplets dripping from the small curls at the nape of his neck, he had just finished washing. He was bent over the trove, giving me the perfect view of his pert ass in his black leather pants. My hands were tingling, and the lower part of me came to life with need. I can't deny that this man sometimes infuriated me, but he wasn't ugly.

"See something you like, Princess?"

I swallowed hard, blinking a few times, then walked over to his side to glance over his shoulder.

"No fucking way! Is that what I think it is?" I asked, excitement filling me as I set my eyes on a batch of—

"Cinnamon biscuits." He finished my thought before I could. In the cast-iron skillet were perfectly golden brown balls of bread with brown swirls of cinnamon baked into it. I reached out to grab one, but he batted my hand away. "You're forgetting which one of us can tolerate heat."

I narrowed my eyes at him. "And you're forgetting that I can handle more than you think I can."

He raised a brow, stood, then backed away. I slowly reached for a bun. The skillet radiated heat, but it wasn't like I hadn't been near a fire before. I was around dragons and they breathe temperatures hotter than this trove. Just before my fingertips could dig into the bread, I reached into my boot and pulled out my blade. As soon as I secured the pommel in my hand, I flipped the blade into my palm and stabbed my food.

When I stood and turned on my heel, I prowled up to my observer and took a single bite, never taking my eyes off him for a second. An uncontrollable moan escaped me as the moistness of the bread and the sweetness of cinnamon brought my tastebuds to life. Those green eyes of his came to life and I saw something in his jaw tick. After swallowing, I licked the sides of my mouth and could've sworn Jaxx growled this time. There was half a bun left, and as I went to bite it again, Jaxx grabbed my wrist and trapped it in his grip again. He slowly brought the bun, still impaled on my blade in my hand, to his mouth and ate the last bite.

He was toying with me as I was with him. When are we going to stop this foolish game we're playing? Part of me wants to drag him to my bed and get it over with it. Then maybe we could focus more on the mission and less on who's going to hold out the longest. We stayed like that for a few minutes after he swallowed. Getting lost in each other's gazes. Repeatedly, this happens to us. And then my heart squeezes as thoughts swirled of what could've been if he hadn't broken the bond before we even formed it.

Jaxx was trying to play the hero.

I didn't want a hero.

I wanted him.

There was a small bite of cinnamon on the corner of his mouth on the right and without thinking to stop myself, I rose onto my tiptoes and licked it. I froze in my spot. In an instant, he pressed my body against his. We were chest to chest, and his mouth was on mine. A mix of cinnamon and Jaxx as our tongues danced. It wasn't a swift and soft kiss, but one filled with longing and need. It had been so long since I last tasted him on my tongue. Felt any sort of passion coming from him into me.

My dagger clattered to the floor. His hands held my hips, and he lifted me, naturally causing me to wrap my legs around him. His skin was warm beneath my touch, and I felt every part of his exposed torso. Starting with his broad shoulder, down his arms, corded with muscle. His lips landed on my neck and my hands explored further, lower, passing his navel and dipping beneath the loose band of his pants. I felt him hard against my palm and, in that moment, I knew I wasn't crazy. Jaxx wanted me just as much as I wanted him.

We never made it past a kiss before he gave his heart up. I rubbed his length up and down as he claimed my lips again. We started moving through the small house until finally landing in the bedroom. My back hit the wall, causing my legs to drop from his waist, and he bent down. My hands rested on his shoulders as our eyes locked. Our kiss left his mouth glossed and bruised. I felt his hands touch the inside of my thighs just above my knees and slowly explore upward.

"Princess, you need to stop me now otherwise…" He stopped, removing his fingers, and waited on his knees in front of me. Abruptly, he stood and turned away, running his fingers through his dark locks. "We can't do this."

"What? Why?" Moving closer to him, I turned him to face me. "Jaxx, what is going on?"

He didn't answer me right away, instead, avoiding my eye. "You shouldn't have kissed me." His words were low. And he almost sounded…angry.

"Excuse me? We've been teasing each other since we met and now you're mad because I finally made a move? After you told me yesterday that if I didn't, you would?"

"That was foolish of me. I only said it because I didn't think you'd be stupid enough to kiss me." His tone was just as harsh as his insult.

My eyes burned, and a lump formed in my throat, but I wouldn't let him do this to me again. "I only kissed you because I figure if we finally fucked, then we would realize there was nothing between us and move on. But I can see that not only was it stupid, but I also want nothing to do with you anymore."

I stormed out of the bedroom, grabbed my packed sack because we were always prepared in case we needed to make a getaway, and made it to the front door before two hands firmly gripped my shoulder, stopping me. Spinning me so hard, I was dizzy until I found his lips on me again. A hand tangled in my hair and his knee thrust between my legs. This was stupid and I should hit. Should yell at him to stop, but when his fingers ran up my thigh, pulled aside my undergarment, and ran two fingers through my pussy, I melted.

It had been so long since someone touched me like this. Since before he touched me like this. And I missed the feel of him. Jaxx's fingers pushed inside of me while his thumb found the small bundle of nerves, rubbing it skillfully. My legs clenched around his thigh as his mouth never left mine. My hands explored his body, and I found the tie on his pants, loosening it until it fell open. I pulled at his pants and he let his knee fall to the floor so my feet were back on solid ground. Jaxx's hand continued to bring me to the edge of bliss as I worked his cock free.

His fingers picked up the pace as I wrapped my hand around his shaft, and I couldn't help but wonder if it would be painful when he entered me. Especially since he was bigger than Tristian and I've never been with anyone else. I moaned into his mouth as he growled into mine. We broke momentarily to look at one another, and when he pinched my bundle of nerves; I screamed. "Jaxx!"

"Hmm." He hummed in approval, then pulled his fingers out of me, bringing them to his lips, licking them clean. "I always knew you were sweet. Now come here, Princess. Let's see how well you ride."

I swallowed hard as I pulled myself toward the settee. He sat down. Then I moved to straddle him, but before I could move my clothing aside, he took one finger and extended the claw into a talon and cut through the garment that was blocking my pussy from his cock. "You'll have to pay for a new one, Jaxx."

He gripped my hip in one hand, then used his other to line himself up with me, but I jumped back. I didn't want to have sex with him for the first time while he didn't posses his heart. "Princess?"

I shook my head from side to side and backed away. Out of instinct, I grabbed my pack and raced out the door, leaving him confused and naked on the settee.

It didn't take me long to make it back into the marketplace. The first person I went to see was the tailor. Her tent, which comprised deep blues and blacks, brought some color to the other white linen tents. She was finishing a trade with another customer and nodded at me when I walked in. I went to the battle skirts. Made of leather from one of the many creatures that lived down here. Like a cow-hide, but that's not what they call them down here. You can't get milk from their tests.

"This one is new," she said as she walked up

beside me.

"I'll take it and the undergarments you made me."

"What happened to the ones you bought two days ago?" Her accent was unfamiliar. A sort of annunciation of each vowel sound.

"Dragon claw tore through one," I answered.

"What do you have for me?" She asked. I never got a name from her. Well, I guess you could say her name was Her or She. She didn't give it out, saying names hold balance and weight in them many don't understand. I respect that, so I didn't question it.

I looked around and then leaned forward to whisper, "Can I work it off?"

She eyed me up and down. "You want to work for me? I thought you said what my girls did wasn't honorable? That they were criminals. What changed your mind?"

Her crossed arms and guarded posture made me nervous, but I answered anyway. "I need to get away from my home for a little while. Send me on a mission. You know I'm a skilled warrior."

Her dark brow rose as she walked closer, scrutinizing me from head to toe. "Aside from your battle and weapon skills, do you know how to seduce others? Make them bend to your will?"

No. "I'm a quick study."

She sighed and looked at the floor before meeting my eyes. "If you wish to be one of my women, then you must have all the skills required."

"I can do it. Please let me prove it. And if I fail, guess what? Sotto will either lock me away or kill me. You will have no connection to me at all." I waited on bated breath for her to answer.

"Cynthia."

A young woman with braided black hair and bright pink eyes emerged from the back slit of the tent. She wore a pink lacey top that was cut off just below her breast, leaving nothing to the imagination, and a floor-length skirt with slits up the sides that exposed her long, golden legs.

"Madam?" Cynthia bowed.

"You must take this one with you on your next mission. Watch her and then report back to me." Cynthia nodded. Madam glanced back at me. "If you complete the mission, then your debt to me will be paid. But if not, then, well, I guess I'll never see you again, anyway."

"Thank you."

I followed Cynthia back to the back, but then Madam said one last thing that stopped me momentarily.

"What do you wish me to tell the dragon when he comes looking for you?"

I closed my eyes and then said, "He won't."

Chapter Fifteen

Jaxx

That didn't turn out the way I expected it, but now I can devour all that fucking breakfast for myself. Which I did, after getting dressed. When I stepped toward the small washbasin in the kitchen to clean my hands, the heel of my boot pressed onto something. Looking down, I sighed, picking up Abbygale's dagger.

She goes nowhere without this one.

I inspected it as the green twine glittered against the black that decorated the hilt. It had a beautiful craftsmanship, but I couldn't recall where she had gained it. When I looked closer, a buzz started forming in my head and a flash happened.

"What's this?" Abbygale asked as I handed her a blade.

"It's for you. I know how you love throwing daggers at things."

"Particularly you," she whispered, and I smiled.

"Just take it, Wildcat." Abby smiled with glee as she grabbed the blade from my hand and tucked it into the back of her right boot. The moonlight was casting a beautiful glow upon her. There would be nothing ever to compare to her beauty, seeing that smile on her face.

I blinked the memory away and gripped my chest as a stabbing pain came and went where my heart used to be. When it was gone, I forced the small blade into my boot to keep it well hidden and exited the house.

I needed a drink.

There was a small tavern just a short distance past the marketplace. Fifty vendors about a half-mile-long stretch. I avoided them all easily marching toward my destination. Inside the extensive building made from brick and motor was a ten-foot bar with various seating throughout. Females and males of all creatures and souls worked and came here to unwind after a long day of work. The workers had different jobs. Some served the drinks, others served the customers with a dance or, if you're feeling lucky, a private show.

"Hello, Jaxx," Cristin Caine hissed as I approached her. Her snake-like tongue slithered out of her mouth as she wiped the bar down. "Your usual?"

"Yeah. Make it a double." I threw down some silver tokens I swiped from a couple of unsuspecting shoppers on the way here.

"Oh, your girl giving you trouble again?" Cristin Caine wasn't just a snake-hybrid, but she was the city's source of secrets. She absorbed them all because blackmail was a tool anyone could use in any position. Did I tell her about the princess? Only that I had a woman living with me. Nothing else. And it wasn't because Abbygale needed protection. It was because my dealings with the princess were exactly that, mine.

"You could say that. Tell me something, Cristin." I tossed an extra coin as she handed me my glass of amber-vain, custom alcohol made from her venom, diluted with homegrown wheat and other ingredients. "How does one go about entering the bogs without having their soul reaped?"

I tipped the glass, relishing in the burn as it went down my throat. "You wish to venture into the Flumen Immortuorum?" I nodded and drained the last of the drink. "There is no way."

"Bullshit. How much will it cost me?" I asked, reaching into my empty pocket on a bluff. Cristin looked around, then leaned across the bar to whisper in my ear. Her tongue sent shivers across my skin, and not effective.

"The only way in and out is to have a soul blocker." When she backed up, we kept eye contact as she continued to speak. "They are extremely scarce. I've only ever heard of one in existence in this realm, but it's impossible to get."

"How much?" Cristin poured me another drink, and I greedily took it, knowing I'd have no way to pay for it.

"It isn't the price you pay, but the risk you take." She turned her back. Meanwhile, I stealthily reached into the drunk man's pocket next to me and grabbed some more tokens. Her venom-infused drinks had caused him to pass out drunk.

"How big is this risk?" I prod.

She sighs, turning to face me once more. "What is so important about those damned bogs? Are you looking to retrieve a lost soul from its depths? Because many have tried, and all have failed. It isn't worth it. Those that are dead should remain that way."

"I'm not looking to save anyone one, Cristin. I just want to see if I can do it."

She sucked her teeth and scoffed, throwing her rag on the bar top. Then, gripping the edge, she shook her head.

"Lord Sotto," she started. "He has one locked up in his palace somewhere. Or so I've been told." Of course, the rich bastard would. "Jaxx, I'm warning you now, if you attempt to break in, you'll die and so will that girl you brought with you."

Cristin doesn't know who we are. I slammed the coins down and hopped out of the stool. "See you around. Thank you for your service."

I exited the tavern with this added information and started plotting how we would steal it on the way back home. I'm sure the princess got over whatever emotions she was feeling and would have dinner ready by the time I got back. If my presence didn't soothe her, then perhaps this news will. One step closer to getting the ashen crown, which means she would be one step closer to getting back to her sister and me getting my revenge.

When I walked inside, an eerie feeling crept up my neck. It was dark and quiet. The faintest smell of cinnamon clung to the air, but that was from this morning. It didn't take me long to realize she hadn't made it back. I shrugged my shoulders and went to the settee. Pulling out some parchment and charcoal we borrowed when we first got here a year ago, I mapped out a plan. I worked on our way in and out, any and every scenario I could think of while waiting for her to return. The sound of the market coming to life again woke me up well past the dawn of light.

She must've snuck past me in the middle of the night. But she couldn't have. I usually wake when I smell her. When I went to inspect her room, I noticed she hadn't slept in her bed at all and her lilac scent was nearly gone. A new feeling rooted itself deep inside of me and I was curious about what it was. I didn't like it one bit. My sense was coming to life as thoughts and images of her being beaten, killed, stolen, or worse, played in my head. I made a quick cleanup of my things and left our apartment. I knew she would go to the tailor if she was running away. Especially after what I did to her clothes.

The Madam greeted me as I entered the tent. She had her long brown hair styled back in a ponytail. The crimson silk of her dress swayed against the rugged floor as she approached me. "Can I help you?"

Her voice was sultry, and eyes were full of secret. "Where is she?"

"I told her you would come looking for her. She thinks the dragon without a heart doesn't care, but she is wrong." Madam approached me. Her eyes scrutinizing me. "A soul doesn't need an organ to guide it to its mate. When the mind and body understand, the heart will follow."

I snarled at her this time. "I care not for your riddles. Where is she?"

Madam smiled, then reached out her hands to me. I flinched back. "Please, let me show you something." I didn't move. "It will bring truth to my words and you will no longer be confused."

"I don't want your magic. I want *her*."

She eyed me curiously, lowering her hands. "The woman does not wish for you to follow. But fear not, dragon, you two will find your way back to one another before the week is over."

"Tell me or I will burn this place to the ground." My green flames sparked to life in my palm.

"For one without a heart, you sure are passionate about her. Is that why you keep pushing her away? Are you afraid she'll restore you?" Madam asked, and I thought for a moment.

"Stop trying to distract me. Where is my princess?" This time I shouted louder than I intended and let my ball of flames fly. It landed on the corner, catching quickly. Smoke consumed the tent.

"Be gone, dragon. You're no longer welcome here." She flipped her fingers, and a burst of ash flavor coated my tongue as I was jolted out of her tent, knocking me backward onto the ground. A crowd stopped for a moment before pressing onward. I leaped to my feet and tried to enter, but a force field caused me to stumble backward. Then, the Madam's voice resounded, "Your princess is stronger than you think, dragon. She does not need you anymore."

A deep growl vibrated in my chest as I turned toward Lord Sotto's palace. It was the largest building in the entire city. If she thinks she gets to steal that damned crown without my help, she is a damned fool. Now I'll have to delay our trip home just so I can save her ass again.

As I walked down the well-worn path of the market, I came across a small bridge that connected the noble lands to our side, the commoners' place, as it was labeled. There wasn't a creek or river separating the two sides but a deep canyon that no one knew just how far into the earth it stopped. There have been rumors that Sotto and the other lords use it for corporal punishment. All crimes against...well, anyone highborn was punishable by death.

Two guards dressed in their simple brown leathers, armed with a single spear each, stood erect as I passed by them. I nodded to them both, stepping onto the soft pea-gravel path that differed vastly from the commoners' clay-dirt ground. I supposed this side wanted to ensure the other needed to know they were the wealthier ones. Compared to the worn down brick and motor buildings, these nearly metal ones appeared richer. Pun intended.

As much as I hated to admit it, I admired some of the beautiful architectural details that went into the frames, some crafted with dragon scales in mind. The sharp petal-like shapes were stacked in perfect asymmetrical designs across the varied rooftops. Even though there wasn't technically a high-sun or white-sun in this realm, the light of day glistened, adding a shimmer to the replicated tops. It reminded me of all the dragons I'd met before being dragged to hell. Verglas was the leader of them all, bonded with Abbygale's sister, Queen Kaleigh Orion.

Then there was Xiong, Verglas's ill-mannered brother, who had a taste for human flesh and bone. As far as I could remember, he had not bonded with a rider yet. I paid no mind to bonding with a dragon, seeing as I had my own wings. Although I longed to stretch them out, but I was lightless here. Not sure what was suppressing my magic, but the sooner I found that crown, the better. I kept them glamoured the past year, only revealing them when we were in the apartment.

Each lord's house sectioned off the rest of this place. Griffin for Lord Ballard, Snake for Lord Caine, Cristin's cousin, and then Lord Sotto, who oversaw the entire city. How he built a democracy in the realm that was always rumored to be where we all went when died was something I'll never understand. Although, I haven't tried to explore further than Umbra Dolor.

Rocks kicked up with the heavy footfalls of my boots as I approached the steps of the enormous palace. Its uniquely shaped columns and onyx-colored material gave it an ominous presence in an even more eerie environment. There was a small drawbridge that was well-protected by four armed guards, just like the other two that greeted me at the bridge. I knew they wouldn't let me just walk in, so I hesitated a moment before the two approached me, crossing their spears to block my path.

"Easy. I just need to speak with Lord Sotto," Isaid, holding my hands up in surrender.

"What is the matter of your issue? The lord isn't seeing commoners today," the one on the right said. He sounded as if he had a tongue caked in chalk.

I racked my brain for an answer, then said, "I know the identity of the person who plans to steal from him."

"You can tell me," he responded.

I shook my head, a slight smirk playing on my lips as I crossed my arms over my chest. "No. I think I'll tell him myself. If he doesn't see me, then he'll never be prepared, and when his precious belongings are stolen, he'll come to you with questions."

I saw the guard swallow and buckle in fear slightly. "Very well. I'll escort you."

As I crossed the threshold, I found myself in a narrow hall illuminated only by torches spaced a few feet apart. There was a strange scent that reminded me of the deserts back in Dalaria. Considering the obvious revenue that has been rolled into this place, it is surprising. I'd imagine it would smell of coin, roasted meats, and wine. Instead, it's a musty, humid tang that lingered in the air. Following me around like my shadow.

At the end of the first corridor, we make a left. There are few changes in our sense of sight-seeing, but as we round another corner to the right, we're greeted by two wide double doors made from none other than metal. My fingers itched to touch them, curious about where and how they got the materials needed to make such fine craftsmanship.

The escort signaled to the other guards to let us pass using some foreign gesture that I couldn't care less about, and we entered a grand ballroom. My boots nearly glided across the smooth, marbled floor, starkly contrasting the pea-gravel outside. It was abundantly clear that this room was built at great expense, as seen from the decorative ceramic columns, pinned crimson curtains, and polished floor. At the front center of the room, like most royals or high-born, sat Lord Sotto.

He adorns himself in all-black leather, with no crown atop his bald head. That differs from any noble I've ever met. Lord Sotto sips on a chalice of wine, I assume, while watching our every step. "Commander?"

Commander? What kind of ranking system makes their leader stand gate duty? "Forgive the intrusion, my Lord, but the man says he has pertinent information for you."

Sotto's yellow eyes move to me. The color reminded me of the high sun at its highest peak. What kind of creature is he? "Speak," he commands.

"This matter is delicate," I said. If I could get him alone, then perhaps I could beat the location of the soul-keeper out of him.

Lord Sotto sighed, then stood to approach me. He stopped just before the toes of his boots met mine and

I'm surprise to find that we are of even size and height. "What is your name?"

"My name is unimportant," I answered, trying to keep my cool.

"Hmm. Did someone die?"

"No."

"Plot to kill me or my family?" Sotto, clearly annoyed and showing no respect for anyone, demonstrated it by invading my personal space. "A rebellion is going to start?" He didn't let me answer him before he tried to grip my neck. My instincts kicked, gripping his left wrist hard and spinning him until his arm was in a position along his back, where I had complete control over him.

"My Lord!" The commander pointed his spear at me, but I turned us so the sharpened end pressed against Sotto's chest.

"I wanted this to be civil, but it's clear to me you think you can do whatever the fuck you want. Not around me, Sotto. And you," I snarled at the commander, visibly quivering in his armor. "What kind of leader brings a stranger into the palace without testing them for weapons and magic? You're a fool."

"I'll have your head for this," Sotto exclaims, so I twisted his arm until I felt the joint pop out of place. He waited in pain, and when I felt his arm go limp, I knew I had complete control. Extending my dragon claws on my right hand, I pressed them into Sotto's chest, batting away the spear before continuing with my threats.

"Tonight, you will host a ball and event for everyone in this city. No matter what family they are born into. You'll invite the Madam to have her ladies here to entertain, all while giving me access to your precious artifact."

"What artifact?" he whimpered.

"You? You're the one plotting to steal the soul-keeper?" the commander shouted.

I smirked, then shrugged while supporting my grip on the lord. "Yes, well, I take more than that. Now, do as I say or else…" I dug my claws in deep, relishing his screams.

"All right!" He wailed. "Yes, Commander, do as he said."

The commander wasn't as foolish as I thought when he nodded and scurried off to follow the orders. "Now, you and I are taking a walk. It's a shame you became so complacent in your position. If the commoners knew how little security you had, they'd have stormed this palace eons ago. How long have you been playing high-lord?"

"You'll never get away with this," he stammered as we approached the back door of the room.

"Unless you're answering my questions or directing me to your little artifact's room, I suggest you keep your insults to yourself. Or your tongue will be the delicacy served during tonight's festivities," I warned. "Now, direct me to where I want to go."

Sotto's good arm moved with much effort as he pointed with a shaky finger toward the door. The same stink and environment greet us as when I first entered the palace. "That way."

Sotto's voice was weak, and it seemed like every word was strained. I followed as he pointed down the narrow corridor to another door. Smaller, we both had to bend slightly to not knock into the top frame. I kept my eyes trained on the path ahead because both sides of us were solid walls. Past the entrance was a short distance walk into a large foyer with three other corridors going in different directions from us.

"Which way?"

"To the far left. That will take us to the vault," he replied, his voice strained and breathless.

Something in my gut was telling me that this was far too easy. Unsure of a trap waiting for me, I pushed him forward, relinquishing my claws just enough to keep control but to let him breathe a little easier. Sotto stumbled as we progressed onward. We stopped just in front of another door. This one differed from the rest, and Sotto let out a heavy wheeze. "I need two hands to open it."

I raised a brow. "Very well."

He wailed when I grabbed his limp hand, raising it. "It requires blood magic." I take out Abby's dagger, press it into each of his palms and aid him in pressing his hands to the door. In a quake of magic, ash filled my mouth just as it always did whenever others practiced. Smoke escaped from the sides like pressure being released from a condensed can. The door slid open and we entered. It was dark, and no time to adjust my eyesight before something sharp stunned me between my shoulder blades. I'm temporarily paralyzed as Sotto rolled forward out of my grasp.

I strained to move, but nothing worked. Sotto spun on his heel to face me. "You shouldn't have come alone. Now you'll be tonight's entertainment. I'll allow my lords to pick their favorite parts off you."

"Or just kill him." It was the commander who suggested that. He came to face me, showing me a silver vial with a long needle at the end. "Pure iron mixed with bone shavings of a dragon. It was a guess what kind of creature you were but, nothing gets past me."

The commander's eyes shifted to bright blue, then back again.

"You're a seer?"

"Not exactly. I'm in the same family. They're more like cousins. I'm blessed with true sight. It gives me the ability to see behind any disguises, magic or otherwise."

"So you saw my wings?" I asked.

"Saw much more than that," he said with a smug look in his eyes.

"If you knew what I was, then why did you let me inside? Why let me hurt your lord?" I needed to know. That way, I could slap myself for being such a fool when I can feel my hands again.

Sotto walked over to the commander, then, with a loud crunching of bones, snapped his shoulder back into place. "Because I told him to bring you to me." Sotto walked over to the far side wall and flicked something. The room came into a light with glittering crystal torches. In the far left corner of the room, I saw something. It was in the shape of a shield with a large ghostly creature imprinted on reminding me of the images of the reapers Mother used to warn me about when I was a child. A glass case was covering it and that's when it clicked for me. "I assume that is what you risked your life for."

I didn't speak.

Sotto walked up to me, his eyes scrutinizing me from head to toe. "What do you want with my soul-keeper? To trade it? Use its magic for a power up? Or is it to return your little side piece to the human realm?"

My eyes narrowed, and Sotto smiled, looking at the commander, nodding. I looked toward the true sight as he pulled something out of his pant pocket—a crumpled piece of parchment with a charcoal drawing on it. Sotto took it, then said, "We've been watching the two of you since you made your way into this realm." He unfolded it. "Did you think I don't know when someone comes into my city?"

Sotto examined the page before turning it over to me, and in perfect imagery was my princess. "She's quite the looker, your little whore. What was her name again, Commander?"

"Abby is what the tavern folks call her," he answered.

"And we have eyes on her, don't we?" The commander nodded. "Last I heard the Madam had taken her in to train her. I wonder if we should invite them to the ball tonight." I wanted to rip his eyes out for daring to look at her. "Yes, that would be most excellent. Here's what I'm going to do before I have you thrown to your death." I felt a tingling return to the tips of my fingers as he continued to gloat. "When I see her, I'll have her escorted to a private room for my pleasuring. If Madam trained her efficiently, she'll be as obedient as the rest. I wonder how her olive skin will look with my hand prints pressed against it? How will she sound when I'm so far buried inside of her? She'll forget you existed?"

"I'm going to rip your tongue for daring to speak of her in that way." Sotto gave a deep belly onechuckle. More feeling returned to my forearms, but I still didn't move.

"Your threats are useless now, Jaxx. You know, I knew your father, Tika. He was a real bastard. Smug because he was the god of dragons, but then a toothpick-sized dragon bone dagger killed him. All for trusting the humans. For sleeping with your filthy mother." I spat in his face, still biding time until the feeling returned completely. Sotto wiped his face while the commander moved to hit me, but the lord stopped him.

"He wouldn't feel it. The paralytic will have him like this for hours," Sotto stated so reassuringly I wanted to laugh.

"You know nothing of dragons or my family. After I rip your tongue, the commander's cock will be next. I'll ensure you choke on it all the while commander will die by one-thousand cuts." This time, I could feel the numbness between my shoulder blades fade.

Just keep them talking a little longer.

"Commander, Lord Sotto, forgive me for intruding, but we need to start the preparations for this evening's festivities." I didn't move to see who was speaking behind me, but Sotto nodded.

"Commander, secure the prisoner. Laura, get the bed chambers ready for this evening. I have a special request for the Madam. I want this one." He stepped to my right, knowing I could see him in my side eye, and handed the lady the image of Abby. The other two disappeared for a moment, then just before the Commander returned with iron cuffs, Sotto leaned into my ear and whispered, "I'm going to make you watch while I ravish her little cunt."

I smirked, then said, "You'll die the second your eyes land on her."

"We'll see."

This entire realm will burn if anything happens to *my* princess.

Chapter Sixteen

Abbygale

Cynthia led me through a narrow slit from the main tent into a back room of sorts. Arranged in a circle, cushions of various colors surrounded a large red carpet at the center. Every cushion was occupied by a woman, aside from two. Cynthia guided me to the center and then spoke. "Madam has wished for Abbygale to join us. We must prepare her for her first mission. Lydia will prep the wash basin with our most pertinent essential soaps and oils. Lacey will handle the cosmetics, Avery the clothing, and I will train her in everything else," Cynthia said, her tone authoritative and confident.

"What is about to happen to me? What mission?" I asked, the instinct to retreat daunting.

"You're about to get a crash course in assassination," she answered.

"I already know how to kill," I reminded her.

Cynthia looked at me from head to toe and then back to my eyes, her gaze flashing a bright blue before she smiled. "You're a human princess with an extensive knowledge of throwing daggers and arrows. What you will learn from us is nothing compared to what your sister tried to teach you."

"How—"

"I'm a true sight, and you're a princess," Cynthia whispered knowingly.

"Like a seer?"

She smiled. "No. Seers get images of the future. I see inside of you. And if you're wondering what I can see in you—you're a true-born princess of the kingdom Orion. Now, I need you to forget everything you know, clear your mind, and pay attention."

I listened intently as Cynthia circled me and then pointed at my clothes, commanding me to undress. Shame or embarrassment didn't wash over me as I followed her. She took my hand, leading me over to the steaming wash basin. An overwhelming scent of florals shook my senses just before the warmth of the water soothed my aching muscles. Pain surfaced in places I didn't know I was hurting. Lydia came to me, washed me like a mother does her babe. It felt nice to be taken care of for once. After my bath, a person took my measurements for a dress like the one Cynthia was wearing. The floor-length black gown hugged my form, exposing my navel with a rhombus shape cut out. Slits in the skirts allowed for easy access to any blade I might hide, but that wasn't the main reason for that design.

It would be to give the customer easier access. I braided my long auburn hair down thc middle and applied cosmetics to my face delicately. Ruby-red pasted across my lips, gold glitter matching the specks in the dress's lace danced across my cheeks while black charcoal lined my eyes, making them pop. Someone handed me a looking glass for my approval, and I didn't recognize myself. It'd been over two years since I looked like a princess.

"What's next?" I asked.

"Now that you're presentable, we will give you the instructions necessary to seduce and kill," Cynthia said.

"I know how to do that," I said, although I've only been intimate with one man and nearly gave myself to…well, he's not important right now.

"Very well, then pretend Lydia is a man. Show us," Cynthia instructed, and I swallowed hard, blinking as Lydia waited for me to act. I prowled slowly forward, like I've seen Jaxx do so many times.

"Stop," Cynthia ordered, and I listened. She came to me, then touched my shoulders. "You're walking like a man. Relax. Us females have the power to entice a man with our bodies. If we approach them like we're stiff, they will turn us away. Watch and learn." I looked where she pointed at Lacey. The young woman walked with ease and grace, her long eyelashes fluttering as she neared Lydia. "You must use your body to flirt. The language we can speak awakens a man's desire more than any word that passes our lips."

Lacey reached out, the middle finger of her left hand softly tracing along Lydia's jaw bone. It was so simple, yet very intimate at the same time. They spoke to each other with their eyes. Every simple touch, brush of their hands, and movement was strategic. It wasn't long before I wanted to master it. "I'd like to try again."

"Very well." Cynthia nodded, and I tried.

Each time I needed correcting.

"Shoulders are too tense," Cynthia commented.

"Eyes are too narrow," Lacey said.

"You aren't moving your hips," Lydia commented as I practiced striding toward her.

"I thought you had to move as if you were riding a

horse? Plus, I don't need to master this position when my intent is not to fuck but to kill," I reminded them.

Cynthia nodded. "But your partner will be very pleased."

"Don't talk to me about Jaxx as if you know us and our non-relationship," I snapped. It wasn't her fault. Jaxx and I were pretty much recluses the entire time we were here. Only leaving our apartment to get supplies or steal from other common folk.

Cynthia's eyes flashed blue for a moment before returning to their natural color. "You lie to yourself too easily, Princess. You will never be ready to perform this mission if you don't release the weight on your chest."

"What, you want me to cry on your shoulder about him? About the fact that he made me fall in love with him so that he could break us?" The well spilled over as the dam inside of me broke. "Jaxx gave his heart to a damn chest rather than to me. And he is so lost that he doesn't realize that I'm not just trying to get the ashen crown to get home to my sister, to kill Rai for everything he has put on my family, my people, though, but to save him as well. Even if it means me dying."

My cheeks were wet, and I could've sworn I saw that charcoal running down my face, messing up the fresh face they all worked so hard to perfect.

"Perhaps Jaxx was doing the same thing you want to do. Sacrificing himself for the one he loves most."

"He didn't ask me. Didn't include me in the decision. How is he my fated mate if he can do those things without seeking my counsel first?" I was a sobbing mess, and I hated it, but the weight on my heart was less.

"Your fated mate, the dragon shifter?" Cynthia asked. I nodded, too ashamed to speak, as I tried to collect myself. "When you go on this mission tonight, think of everything and use that to focus."

"What is my mission?" I finally dried my face. Lydia grabbed my hand while she and Lacey went to work fixing the mess I created.

"If you wish to retrieve the ashen crown from the bogs, Madam will give you the information, but you must assassinate the lord this evening, or she will not let you keep the soul-keeper," Cynthia warned.

I stood and faced her. "The soul-keeper will protect me when I'm in the bogs?" She nodded. "Then I'll do what must be done."

It took the rest of the afternoon before I had some inkling of seduction. They fitted me with thigh holsters to carry two daggers, and I realized mine was back at the apartment. It was the only weapon Jaxx ever gave to me. But I wouldn't let that sentiment distract me. He was busying himself with tavern women while I focused on getting us home.

When I was ready, with my matching half-face mask secured to my face, I followed the girls to the stables outside the tent. I didn't realize there were horses here, although they didn't look like the stallions back home. They have four ears. The top is larger than the bottom, with three eyes and six legs. This realm will never cease to amaze me with its unique creatures. Attached to two of them was a carriage. We all got inside, then just as we were about to be whisked away, Madam came.

"Cynthia, I need to speak with you a moment." We all waited as Cynthia received whispered words from the leader of this party. Madam approached me as Cynthia took her seat beside me and looked deep into my eyes as if she was trying to reach my soul. "Be brave, be fierce, and be aware, Princess."

I nodded just as the carriage took off.

The ride was rough, going from the sand-packed path of the commoner's place, crossing the bridge until the wheels hit the pea-gravel of the wealthy side of this city. We nearly come to an abrupt halt on the other side while the guards check the caravan of carriages for weapons and invite. I adjusted my matching silk robe that Cynthia gave me, and she squeezed my hand, reassuring me that the guards would not detect my tiny blades. I guess it depends on how thorough the security is.

We finally made it to the castle without further delay. As someone pointed us towardthe entrance, Cynthia handed the carriage to a waiting valet. We follow the flow of the crowd, and I can see that we're the only four dressed in the immodest fashion. It's a wave of humidity and wealth; we're the standard that interrupts beauty. I swallow down any doubt and go ahead with caution.

Judging by the dullness of the corridor that led us here, I never would've expected it to be so polished. The place was overflowing with people. Some mingled in clusters while others danced to the rhythm of a string quartet playing at the center front. "There is the lord. He is your target."

My gaze followed Cynthia's to the bald man sitting on the throne scrutinizing his guests. "I'm on it."

Cynthia stopped me momentarily, her hand slipping something into mine with a silent warning dancing in her eyes and a notion of luck. I made my way to the front, stealthy, stopping every few feet to let the other lords and ladies admire me. If I was to appear to be eager, Lord Sotto might consider me desperate, which Lydia recommended that I not do.

"You're looking delectable tonight." I smile and flutter my eyelashes as a blonde-masked man greets me.

"You flatter me, my Lord." I flashed him a smile, puffed out my chest slightly so that he can see the valley of my breast.

"Is your first dance taken?" he asked.

I'm about to say something, but a sudden drum roll silences the room. We turn to face the front, my shoulder brushing against his biceps. Lord Sotto rose to address the room. "Good evening. What a wonderful sight it is to see all my people in one place. I know it was strange to invite my common folk, but alas, it was time to show that I don't favor the highborn. Tonight, you're all in masks. Take this chance to have fun. Be brave. Do something reckless while no one knows who you are. But remember to flee the bed before the other rises in the morning."

A roar of laughter echoed through the room, and I had to force a smile.

"Settle down. Settle down." The people listened, and then four guards burst through the door, escorting a prisoner in chains. A large sack was over the man's face, but I could see it was a dragon shifter. The bone tips of the large wings drug across the floor, and a ten-pound weight dropped in my stomach.

Jaxx? No, it can't be.

"I have some entertainment for you all tonight.

Recently today, my commander and I captured a treasonous thief as he tried to steal my most precious artifact and kill me." Lord Sotto walked over to the prisoner, gripped the sack, and lifted it to reveal him. Rage took over. Knife wounds littered his face, arms, and anywhere I could see cuts in his clothes. Being down here weakened Jaxx, but something else suppressed his power, similar to the iron dust in Shulong.

My hands curled into fists so hard I knew my nails would leave half-moon impressions against my palm. I moved again of my volition as Sotto continued to speak. "Tonight, he will die by one thousand cuts. Commander and the army have him up to five hundred. And I believe we have another five hundred in attendance tonight. So, you will take this dragon bone dagger and your meat. Anyone who refuses will suffer the same."

The crowd murmured their differing opinions until a cheer broke out, and the unanimous death sentence rang loud and true.

"What are you doing?" Lacey rushed to my side to stop me in my path.

"Killing him." I gestured to Sotto.

Lacey shook her head from side to side as a strike line formed. It made me feel sick to see it, and I felt like the porridge I ate this morning might come back up when they made the first cut. Jaxx didn't even scream. His eyes were weary. Limbs hung loose in the chains that bound him to the brick wall. "Not yet, Princess. Remember that saving him is not your goal tonight." I shot a glare in her direction.

"Don't worry, Lacey. Before this evening is over,

everyone who touched him will be dead." When I started my kill list a year ago, Rai was number one, but now Sotto has taken that spot.

I left Lacey where she was standing as I forced my way to the front. Considering he was currently watching Jaxx's sentence being carried out, getting Sotto's attention wouldn't be difficult. When my left foot touched the first step to the small platform, guards halted me in my place.

I whispered in a low tone, blink brightly at the men just as I was taught, and convey, "The Madam has sent me."

When I caught Sotto's gaze, he smiled. "Let her through."

I loosened my muscles, although that proved more difficult now that I was face to face with the man who had just sentenced my...partner to death.

Sotto was watching my every move. The way my hips swayed, arms hung loose at my sides, and the smooth approach kept him in a trance. Sotto stood when I stopped in front of him. His eyes assessed me from head to toe with a slow, victorious smirk on his pale face. Of course, he would be the only one not wearing a mask. "Hello, my dear, you're one of Madam's newest recruits." It was a statement more than a question.

"Yes, my Lord," I responded, my words sounding like velvet, and strained as I tried to keep my composure.

"Well, let me look at you. Twirl." I was going to twirl my blades deep into his fat chest. But I needed to be smart. Releasing a breath, I did as I was told. When I came to face him once more, he pulled me into his lap, forcing us to sit. With one hand holding a chalice of drink, he gripped my hip with the other.

"Does my appearance please you?" I asked, sounding like a naïve schoolgirl.

Sotto's eyes drifted to the exposed cleavage, then back to my eyes. "Very. Now, I want to watch my prisoner die, then you shall be my just reward."

"Reward for murder and torture?" I quipped, then bit the inside of my cheek.

"You disagree with my sentencing? Tell me, what would you have me do to someone that tried to steal from me? Attempted to take the life of your lord?"

The ball of insults in my throat went down hard when I swallowed.

I slipped from his lap, deliberately trailing my hand up his inner thigh before walking over to where he had Jaxx. A guard moved to step in, but Sotto was at my side, waving them off. I leaned down in front of him. Sweat, blood, and small bits of flesh drenched and matted his black curls. My heart thundered in my chest as I took another breath to control my anger. His head was hanging low, eyes closed, so he didn't know it was me.

"Why did you commit treason?" I asked aloud, but Jaxx didn't answer. I needed him to look at me. To know that I was here and I would not leave this place without him.

Sotto used his free hand to jerk Jaxx's head until his neck was taut. "The woman asked you a question."

Jaxx's right eye opened while the left eye remained swollen shut.

"Hello, what is your name?"

Did he recognize my voice? My scent?

His emerald eye was not as bright as it usually was.

Sotto was killing him slowly, and I feared that if I didn't act soon, I'd lose him. "Leave…me…to…die."

Jaxx's words came out with a heavy exhale.

"How many more cuts until he is dead?" I asked Sotto.

He shrugged.

"Give me the honor of killing him." I stood and placed one hand on Sotto's cheek, then the other over his already harden cock. Bile rose in my throat, but if I needed to touch him to get him alone, to get him to do what I wanted him to do, then so be it. Sotto smiled a surprisingly white smile. "I'll show you pleasure you've never experienced before in your entire life."

Sotto smiled. Then his free hand let go of Jaxx, snapped to the back of my neck, then pulled me into his hot lips. It took every fiber of my being not to push him away. I could easily bite his tongue off, but I had to keep up pretenses. "Very well. Bring the prisoner to my chambers."

The plan was in-action, and I knew once we entered his bed chambers, there would be no turning back.

Chapter Seventeen

Jaxx

I've never felt this weak in my entire life. Even when Rai had that traitor bitch Alma use suppressants on me. Or even when Abby and I were in those caves finding the damned chest that held the dagger needed to kill the dark wizard. That was because none of the iron was mixed with dragon bone. The guards must carry me four at a time. Pain erupts from the bone tips of my wings throughout my body. Each slice of the blade and poke of the needle filled with dust made from iron takes my soul further from the light.

Would this kill me?

Do I care?

Sotto and his concubine walk inside, clasping iron chains to a chair and binding me to it. I didn't care to look at her. Anyone loyal to him is an enemy to me.

"Shall I put on a show?" the woman asked, her voice having a tang of familiarity, but I wouldn't know where I could've seen her. A patron of the tavern or even the market.

Someone, a guard I think, pulls my hair out of my face to force my gaze to meet them. If I could, I would avert it, but someone clasps a collar around my neck. I'm being treated like some kind of animal.

"I don't think so," Sotto replied. He pulled the girl

by her hand, leading her toward me. "The Madam has sent you here to please me. To give me anything I want." The woman nodded as if he asked her a question. I blinked my one good eye as Sotto placed the dragon shone dagger in her hand. "Kill him."

She physically baulked before stepping backwards. Sotto was too quick, grabbing her wrist, then forcing it up the middle of her back like I did to him. "I will not kill him." She snapped. "And you can't make me."

Sotto snarled, then ran a tongue along her neck. Deep blue eyes connected with my one opened one. A small fire blazed and I watched as the woman pulled a small blade from beneath her skirts with her free hand. Then there was a single stab. Sotto's eyes widened as he left go of the woman to hold the gash on his neck. There's only one woman I know that can be that precise and sneaky with a blade.

"My Lord!" The two guards in the room came charging toward them. One attacked her, while the other raced to help his master. "You'll die for this."

The woman unmasked herself, then drew the other hidden blade, before saying, "If you don't free him, then you'll be in a grave next to him."

"Abby." She didn't look at me. Not letting herself get distracted, the guard stabbed at her stomach, which she dodged, rolling out of the way while extending both arms and slicing at the guard's unprotected legs. He wailed, falling forward, and catching himself just before me. Abby was quick to slice his throat, blood spurting all over me, the floor, and herself. She swiped the keys off him, paying no mind to the other guard running off to find more help.

"You shouldn't have come for me," I told her as

she unlocked each wrist. "They'll be out for blood now."

The collar fell to the floor and Abby caught me, lifting my head to meet her eyes. Those lips of hers pressed into mine, and that stupid hole in my chest sparked to life once more. "Don't worry, Dragonboy, I'll get you all fixed up once we escape."

If I could smile without hurting, I would. Abby walked over to the case after I stumbled to the bed to help lift myself. She tried to break the case, but I knew it needed Sotto's magic. "Use his blood."

Abby nodded and walked over to the now-deceased lord. She gripped his arm and dragged him across the room, leaving a pool of crimson in her wake. I watched in awe as my wildcat, my princess, my…mate, smeared blood on Sotto's limp hand before pressing it against the case. Ash filled my mouth at the use of magic before the glass container lifted. Quickly, Abby lifted the soul-keeper from its pedestal and scrambled to me. I placed an arm around her shoulder, trying to will my wings away, but I was too weak.

"I'll support you, but we have to get out of here."

I nodded.

We moved as quickly as we could throughout the corridors. Both trying to remember how we got into the room.

Once we reached the outside steps, I realized it must have been a side entrance because there were no guards in sight. A well-worn path led to a brackish branch forest. I could only assume was a part of Umbra Dolor, and we were off. We made it into the forest a few yards before shouts erupted at our rear. Glows of lit torches illuminated shadows of guards. Howls of wolf packs echoed throughout.

"We have to find shelter." Abby hurriedly started while we kept moving. I knew I was only slowing her down. If I stopped, then perhaps they would take me, and she could get away.

"Leave me." It came out whispered and she kept looking high and low, west and east for anything that would shelter us. "Leave me."

I lifted my arm from her shoulders, putting a foot or two gaps between us.

"What are you doing?" she asked, concern blooming in her eyes.

"Take the soul-keeper, find the ashen crown, go home and kill Rai," I said.

She scoffed, shaking her head before closing the gap again. Her hands cupped my face. She rose to the tips of her toes then kissed me hard again. I felt her tongue pressing against the seam of my lips and I let her in. My arms wrapped around her, my body coming to life with need and desire for her.

In this moment, I knew it didn't matter if I had my heart because I would belong to her.

"Wildcat," I warned.

"Stop talking," she demanded, beginning to reach for the waistband of my pants.

"For the great king's sake, will you stop and listen to me?" I almost shouted. Abby looked at me, retracting her hands and backing away.

"Is this because I rejected you first?" she asked, her voice breaking. In the moon's light, I saw just how beautiful she was. It wasn't the new hair or paint on her face, or even the gods' damned dress, but her. Now I knew why fate had picked her.

"Oh, Wildcat, if you think you are turning me down for a quick fuck would make me never want you, you've lost your goddamned mind." Abby balked in a very adorable manner.

She crossed her arms over her chest, unintentionally making some of her cleavage bust out of that skimpy dress. "Jaxx, I don't want to just be some fuck girl to you. We were…" She stopped, shaking her head. "It doesn't matter. You're right. We should keep moving until we reach a safe place. Then regroup in the morning."

"No, Wildcat. You must keep going."

She started shaking her head, stepping into me. I gripped her face, looking into her eyes, that well with a mix of emotions. "No, Jaxx, I just witnessed you being repeatedly cut after it was evident that you were tortured and beaten. We do this together, or not at all."

I brushed a single strand out of her face.

The pounding of paw steps, the howling of the pack, and the shouting of the guards made my ears twitch. "Leave, *now!*"

Abby spun on her heel, daggers at the ready in her hand as she shielded me. "Damn it, Wildcat, retract your claws and scamper off." She looked over her shoulder, smirking at me with defiance dancing in her eyes. Before I could take a hold of her, she was racing into danger.

"Princess!"

"See if you can keep up, Dragonboy!" She knew I could not. Not in the state I was in. My wings were heavy, and I could barely lift them as I looked for something I could use as a weapon, but there was nothing.

I followed her because regardless of how I felt, she would not be doing this alone. The closer I got to her, the louder the shouts came. Growls from the hounds. Then there were whimpers. I moved faster, trying to pump my arms and will my legs to run. My heightened senses started becoming empowered again as the iron dust slowly wore off. I could hear metal clashing with metal, screams of pain and anguish mixed with the increased rush of blood in my ears.

My one good eye zoomed in and out, my long-distance vision blurring. It took me a few more sprints before I finally came upon her. I glued my gaze to the scene playing out in front of me. Her mahogany brown hair danced in the wind as her braids fell loosely across her shoulders. The movement of her body flowed easily as the waves of the sea against the shore. In this very moment, pure admiration for her strength paralyzed me, not with fear or restraint.

Unconcerned by the blood soaking her, she moved across the lines and stabbed the guards in the most precise spots on their necks. The hounds would not go near her for fear that she, the hunter, would kill them next. There was one guard left out of the twenty that came for us. I made my way slowly to her as she placed the edge of the blade against his throat.

"Please, I'll do anything," he begged.

"You honestly think I had let you live after what you put my mate through? After thinking you could get away with hurting him?" She did not let him protest any longer. Her eyes locked with mine as I stood behind the guard. When she sliced the blade across his skin, I fell head over heels in love with her.

"We're safe for now, but the sooner we get that

crown, the sooner we can go home," she said.

"The beauty in you is undeniable." I was not sure what power this was to make me feel this way about her when I had since lost my heart, but it did not matter. I stepped toward her, taking her hips in my grip before whispering in her ear, "I'm going to fuck you now."

She shuddered beneath my touch, and I did not wait for her to protest. My lips claimed hers in a needy kiss. Our tongues danced as I lifted her, letting her wrap those thighs around me. Her back pressed against the nearest tree, and I set her legs down, dropping to my knees. I lifted her left leg, resting the heel of her shoe on my shoulder before trailing my fingers up her leg to where her undergarment was already damp. Extending a claw, I tore it away like last time. I needed to taste her.

Her skirts came over me as I dipped my head between her thighs, running my tongue against her pussy, pleased with the sound she made while her hand gripped my hair. "Ride my tongue, Princess. Show me how wild you truly are."

"Jaxx," she moaned, her hips beginning to move across my face like I told her to. I used one hand to keep a hold on her leg and the other to play with her clit. Teasing that bundle of nerves while sticking two fingers inside of her. I wanted to fuck her already, but as I was claiming her to be my mate, I needed her permission. I picked up the pace, pumping my fingers in and out, her grip on my head tightening. Her hips moved faster, matching my pace.

"Come for me now, Wildcat." My teeth nipped her clit, and she shuddered against me. I licked her clean before she had me on my back, against the dirt. Her hands fumbled with my waistband, but I helped her, and my cock sprang free. She licked my shaft from bottom to tip and wrapped that taut mouth around the head, sucking the life out of me. "Wildcat, wait."

She blinked at me, then paused. "What? Am I doing something wrong?"

I sat up, taking her into my lap so her wet pussy could grind over my cock. She moaned. "Not at all but I want to feel us, skin to skin. No clothes on when we come together. Being my mate and me claim—"

"Mate? You are claiming me as your mate *now?*" she asked, almost baffled.

I sighed. "I know you are thinking how I could be your mate without my heart, but when you killed Sotto for me, my soul, my dragon soul, reached out. I'm not entirely sure how this kind of soul magic works, but I imagine being fated has to do with our souls, not our hearts."

Abby blinked, then nodded. "You have me, Jaxx. You have had me since the first moment I laid eyes on you."

She kissed me deeply. "You have had me since you pressed the tip of the blade to my neck, Wildcat. Now, I need your permission to make it official."

"You have it, Jaxx. I am yours forever."

"Then let us do this right. You deserved to be worshiped, but not in the dirt covered in blood. When I finally have you naked and in my bed, I am going to taste every inch of you." Her hips moved as her wetness rubbed against my beating cock. Gods, if she did not stop, I would bend her over and fuck her right here, right now.

"Jaxx," she moaned, her hands going over her

breast to the clasp of her dress, releasing it. I damn near came at the sight of her. My mouth watered, and I leaned forward, claiming one nipple into my mouth and sucking. "Fuck, I need you right now."

I lifted my head to look at her. "You deserve better."

She shook her head, then stood, letting the rest of her clothes slip off. Abby held out her hand to me. I took it, and she helped me out of my pants, peppered my legs with kisses, and urged me to remove my shirt. I let her guide me to the makeshift pallet she made with our clothes, and then sat. She came over to me, posting herself above me, then gripped my cock, lining herself up and sinking all the way down. We both moaned in pleasure but did not move yet.

Abby kissed me gently, taking my hands and placing one on her right hip, the other on her left breast before she rode my cock. "This is perfect, Jaxx. I would not want to be anywhere else than right here, with you, underneath the starless sky."

There was a dim glow that illuminated from the sky, but I didn't care about anything else than the beautiful woman making love to me. Our lips locked and I could not stop myself from bringing her closer to me. The heat of our skin moving against each other in a tangle of limps. I found her bundle of nerves again, bringing her to another climax before rolling us over and plunging deep inside of her.

My pace picked up, our eyes locking as I felt my soul reaching out to hers, connecting, and when I brought us to the edge again, I let go, claiming her mouth once more.

We did not stop after that. If I was not tasting her

on my tongue, I was deep inside of her.

When we lay in each other's arms, kissing until our lips were sore, Abby leaned forward to whisper in my ear, "I love you, Jaxx. I am in love with you and there is nothing in this realm or the next that I would not do for you."

I believed that with my entire being. When I looked deep into her ocean-blue eyes, I cupped her cheek. "Thanks for saving me, Wildcat."

"I'd burn the world down if it meant rescuing you."

Chapter Eighteen

Abbygale

Pure bliss took over as Jaxx's body came together with mine. His lips perfectly fit against mine, wings cocooned us in our own bubble of ecstasy. This moment with him was everything I wanted and more. My heels dug into his ass, urging him to move deeper, nails dug into the thick skin of his shoulders—I needed him closer to me. I wanted him to consume me completely.

"Jaxx," I moaned as he bit into my neck, sucking hard enough to leave a mark, *his* mark. He brought us closer to the edge again, and with our hands together, we jumped. Our whispered words of love, breaths of air between us. Jaxx pulled me into him, keeping one of his wings over us as if to shield us from sight.

His fingers moved in calming circles across my navel, and I was happy. My body was more relaxed than it had ever been. "I never want this moment to end."

"Hmm. Me too, Wildcat," he whispered. "But you wish to go home, and I wish to kill Rai."

"And restore your heart," I added, and he nodded. His silent agreement did not make me feel any better, but some battles are not worth fighting. "Then I suppose we should get started. I imagine another hunting party will come looking for this one."

"Perhaps we should find a place to bathe." He rolled over to face me, then moved my body on top of his. My pussy landed on his soft cock and it made me want him again. I moved my hips up and down. My nipples hardened, and when his eyes glossed with desire and hunger, I knew we would not be leaving without fucking again.

Jaxx shot up, one hand gripping my hair and the other moving between us to line up his cock. I plunged down onto him, my lips connecting with his in a hurried kiss. It was quick, but still perfect. My body molded to his and the rhythm of our bodies moved perfectly in-sync. I thought about the future. Would we have children? Is that something I should be concerned with since we were not using any kind of contraceptive?

I hesitated, unsure if I should ask Jaxx about demigod birth control methods, but as we got dressed and began our trek back toward the city, the fear of his reaction kept me silent. "Jaxx, what exactly does it mean to be your mate?"

He smiled at me in that boyish way he always did, then said, "Oh, Princess, it means that the world will die if it hurts you. If anyone ever lays a hand on you, the trees will burn, the animals will be slaughtered, and every creature, human or otherwise, will be destroyed. Tongues will be ripped from mouths that dare to insult you, and…" He pulled me into his chest. "We fuck anytime, anywhere."

"But what about our future? Are we married? How come we don't have a symbol like Emnera and Calian?"

Jaxx shrugged his shoulders. "Marriage isn't

something that has ever crossed my mind, and I don't need some magical embellishment to tell me who I love."

I knew he meant that to reassure me, but I cannot shake the feeling that this is more one-sided. "And children? Are you using some kind of contraceptive to prevent me from getting pregnant?"

"No. Why should you worry about that? If you are a wild child, I would think it would be a blessing."

"Jaxx!" I wrenched myself free from him and took the lead, needing to distance myself. My stomach churned with sickness. Oh, great kings of the past, what if I am with child already? Stupid, I was such a fool to think this union between us meant more to him than just a mating ritual. Gods, I am an idiot.

"Wait up," he hollered, but I kept my pace.

"Keep up. If you can fuck me over and over, then you should be healed enough to match my pace," I shouted over my shoulder.

The walk was silent the rest of the way. We did not try to touch one another, which made small little balls of regret form in my stomach. As we made it out of the woods and back to the side entrance of the palace, the goal was to steal some clothes to make it back to the Madam's tent. I knew she would help us, considering I killed Sotto.

There were still no guards watching the side door, and we went back inside. Keeping to either side of the wall, we traced our steps to Sotto's chambers. From there, taking the corridors out of the front gate and across the bridge.

"Jaxx…" I paused, looking around. "It's too quiet."

He stood on my left. "They are all sleeping."

I shook my head. "No. Something is wrong."

"Let's just make it to Madam's. If anything is amiss, she will know."

Jaxx took the lead, but I pulled my tiny blades out to ensure I was ready for anything. When we made it to the edge of the market, it was even more unusual. The normal buzz of the patrons and vendors was gone. Nothing remained. Not a single tent.

"What happened?" I asked aloud.

"Stay behind me, Princess."

I rolled my eyes at him before making my way down the path. Madam's would not be too far of a walk from where we stood. I kept my head on a swivel, looking all around us and even into the skies. We stopped just outside the tent, but it was also too quiet. When I went inside, I was not prepared to see the horrible scene laid out before me.

"Oh, gods." Lacey's head was hanging from a spike while her arms were pinned to the tent wall alongside Lydia and Madam's. The rest of their bodies were chopped into pieces at the center of the main tent.

The only person I did not see was...

"Abby?"

"Cynthia!" I rushed over to her. Kneeling on the floor as she hung on to life. Her eyes were drifting close, and I assessed her for injuries but saw nothing external. "Are you okay?"

"I...I don't know. They killed them, but they left me alive."

"Why did they do this?" I asked, my voice cracking with emotion.

Cynthia investigated me, our eyes connecting as she responded, "They wanted to send you a message."

"Who?" I lifted her head onto my lap, and Jaxx came to sit beside me, handing me a cup of water.

"The commander and Sotto's wife." She sat up further, sipping slowly, and I was feeling relieved that she did not appear injured aside from the bump on her head.

"He was married?"

She nodded. "Lady Sotto knew of his extracurriculars, but didn't care because she had her own indulgences." I raised a brow, and she drained the cup. "You must know, Princess, that she seeks what you do, but for nefarious reasons."

"The ashen crown? She is going after it? But how can she go into the bogs without the soul-keeper?"

"I don't know, but she told me this. You will pay the price for killing her husband and the father of her children. Blood will have blood," Cynthia said. "But I think I can help you get the crown before her."

"How?" I wondered because without the soul-keeper, there would be no way to safely go into the bogs. And what did the lady want with the crown? "What can the ashen crown truly do?"

Cynthia looked at me, then to Jaxx. "It can give the monarch unimaginable gifts. But, the legend goes that the crown will reveal the truth of this realm. Only those that belong here are permitted to stay. The depths of the bogs will claim your soul and reduce your body to ash if you are false. This realm will bear no false crown."

I got the feeling there was more she was not telling us, but if she could help lead us to the bogs, then the rest would surely work itself out. While at Madam's, I separated myself from them to take a bath and find some new clothes. The warm water washed over me

143

like silk. My eyes remained closed as I tilted my head back. Something warm came over me. Another pair of familiar lips masked with the spiced scent of Jaxx.

He broke away, only to climb into the bath behind me. His fingers dug into my shoulders, his cock pressing against my back as I relaxed against him. "What's on your mind, Wildcat?"

"You don't want to know," I whispered.

"Hmm. How do you know if you don't share it? If there a dilemma I could help you solve?"

There is, but now wasn't the time to worry about future nonsense when tomorrow was never promised. I spun around to face him, then straddled him. Not wanting to talk, but to distract myself. Using Jaxx to escape my thoughts, my responsibilities, even for a moment. I sank down onto him. The water sloshed around us as I rode his cock. My breast rubbing against his chest and he caught my mouth with his. One of his hands moved to my clit as he circled it, while the other grasped my ass.

His fingers played with the puckered hole, and I shivered at the thought. It was unexplored territory, but I did not care if he wanted to try. I slowed down to a more causal pace, then looked into his emerald eyes. "Do it."

He raised a brow and pushed the tip of his finger inside. "More?"

I nodded, then kissed him harder as he slowly pushed his finger inside of me. It burned at first. I felt full with his cock in my pussy and his finger in my ass. I picked up my pace and so did he, matching it. "More, Jaxx."

He added a second finger. "I'm going to come,

Princess. Fuck, you're everything I wanted and more."

"Jaxx!" I clenched down on him, but his fingers did not stop fucking my ass as I rode out my climax.

"I need to keep prepping you, Wildcat. If you ever want me to fit." My pussy tightened around his cock. "I have a salve I can use to help lubricate."

"Don't stop. I'm going to come again." I moaned into his chest as my head fell forward.

"Fuck, I won't last much longer if you keeping clenching around me." He pulled his fingers out and got up, pulling me with him. I dried off and then laid on the bed of pillows, waiting for him to return. He had gone into another part of the tent and returned with a tube in his hands.

He crawled over me, kissing me. "Turn over."

I did as I was told, getting on all fours, and waited. He rubbed a cold and gel-like substance against my ass. Jaxx rubbed his cock up and down before stopping to push forward. "Jaxx, just get it over with, fuc—" He pushed forward all the way to the hilt. I felt his balls pushing against my pussy and I caught my breath.

"Talk to me, Princess." There was so much concern in his voice.

"Fuck me, Jaxx. I want you to come inside of me."

"You don't have to ask me twice." His fingers dug into my hips as he kept a punishing pace. My hand went to my pussy, playing with my clit, adding more pleasure to compensate for some of the pain. I knew it would hurt, but after this, if we did it again, it would get better.

Right now, the pain kept all thoughts of the future at bay. I focused on the feel of him moving in and out. The smell of his natural spiced scent and the feel of my soul wanting to connect with his.

He picked up the pace, and then pulled me up to kiss me. Gripping my breast while fucking me into oblivion. "I love you, Wildcat."

"I love you too." A single tear was shed from my eye as he came inside of me.

We fell to the pallet of pillows, and he gently pulled out. Grabbing a wash rag, he cleaned me first before turning to wipe himself down. I did not stay laying down, needing to get away from him before I broke down. After quickly getting dressed, I excused myself to the main tent where Cynthia was reading lore books on this realm. The bodies were gone as Jaxx had left to help her burn them.

I knelt beside her, careful to avoid sitting after the punishment my ass had just endured. "You smell of sex, Princess. Did you let the dragon claim you, yet?" Cynthia kept reading, and I ignored her. "Has his symbol appeared on your chest along with yours?"

I wanted to look but again, just kept pretending to read over her shoulder. "Avoiding my questions will only prolong the truth."

"I think you should keep my sex life out of your thoughts and on the plan."

Cynthia sighed, then closed the book to look at me. "A distracted warrior is just as useless as a novice. You must tell me what is on your mind. I am a true sight, remember?"

She was right. As annoying as it was to admit. "Fine. Jaxx and I have consummated several times, but nothing magic has happened except the orgasms."

"I see. And, has he claimed all of your body?"

"Yes. Just now, if you must know."

"And it was…?"

"Magical. Yes. I let the dragon fuck me in all my holes and it was amazing, okay? Still does not mean I'm his mate or whatever." I sighed.

"Yes, it does." I raised a brow. "Listen, a demigod claims their mate by filling them with their seed in any way possible. It is how they ensure their line will continue." She paused. "Yes, babies. If you are not with child yet, you soon will be."

I stood, looking at her in disbelief and shaking. "No. No. No. I thought we had to have a bond and be married. I am not ready for motherhood. There is still so much I need to learn about him."

"Well, I can look if you wish."

"What does that mean, exactly?" I asked, and she gestured for me to sit with her. "I can see if the seed is making progress inside of your womb."

"Umm, so you have like the ability to see inside of my body?"

She nodded.

"That's creepy."

"What did you think I meant when I said I could see your soul? Just as the Madam could."

"Not that. I thought you meant figuratively or an aura or something. Not inside of me."

"Do you want me to look or not?" she asked, sounding flustered.

I bit my lip, trying to think about it, but then decide it is best not to dwell on something that is uncertain. "No. I just want to know how to get this crown, kill Rai, and restore his heart. My future is only focused on those things."

"Very well, Princess."

She flipped the book open and read. It was filled with a language I did not understand. "What does this all mean?"

"Well, it says that to active the soul-keeper, one must let it borrow their soul. It essentially keeps it safe while the mind and body go into the bogs. The ashen crown rests on the head of the first ruler of Immorteum. When the rightful king or queen places the crown upon their head, the powers of Immorteum will flow through them. You will bend the rift between the living and the dead, which means you could go back home."

"What about killing Rai? He seems immortal," I asked.

"I'm not sure, but it says that you would be immune to all magic except Emnera's, as her light in the darkness is opposite of the ashen crown." Cynthia looked at me and I thought about that.

"Can Emnera help bring me back to the light if I were to wear it and succumb to the darkness?"

"That would be an example. You speak as if you know the goddess."

"We are friends. Long story for a different time."

"Okay. And I assume you wish to know how to restore Jaxx's heart?" I nodded. "Well, the chest requires blood magic and a sacrifice to be made. So, all you need is his blood to open the chest, but another must take his place; otherwise, the chest will kill him. And if you destroyed the chest, the person's heart that was last inside would die with it."

"Thank you, Cynthia."

"Do not thank me until you have won. The journey will not be easy, Princess. And you must not let your feelings and doubts about Jaxx stop you from loving him while you can." Her tone went from friendly to warning in a matter of seconds.

"What does that mean?" She did not speak. "Is something going to happen to him?"

"I cannot say for sure, but all this magic is risky. You could retrieve the crown and live a happy life with him here. Perhaps if you gave Lady Sotto the crown, she would pardon you both."

"Are you crazy? I am not staying down here. My place is in Orion on my sister's side, not down here with souls that are dead or tortured."

"You seem like you would fit in perfectly."

What does that mean?

I shook the confusion from my head and then walked away from her. "We leave tomorrow morning. Be ready."

Chapter Nineteen

Jaxx

"What is something you wish to have once all of this is over with?" I asked Abby as her naked body laid pressed against mine. Cynthia let us use this back tent as a private quarters and I appreciated it. My wings flexed, and I was healing surprisingly quickly. Even with all the fucking.

"I wish to be free, Jaxx," she whispered.

"Free of what?" I was not sure if she meant responsibilities or me.

She turned to face me, tears shedding as she spoke the words into the universe, "Of everything. You included."

I swallowed the lump that formed in my throat, then nodded. "Then it will be done."

She had never been this full of emotion before but I let her cry all night in my arms until she fell asleep. I slipped from the pallet, pulling the cover over her before wearing my pants to go outside for some air. It was oddly quiet, and I was curious if Lady Sotto had brought the entire city with her but that couldn't be possible.

"They were all taken by her." I glanced over to see Cynthia coming out with her shawl draped over her shoulders. "The people. I know you are curious about what happened to them and you should be. She took all their souls with her to use as sacrifices to the reapers, hoping they would bring her the ashen crown."

"What? Did you tell Abby?" Cynthia shook her head as she prowled toward me. Her night dress leaving nothing to the imagination.

"Just like I did not tell her of the many nights we spent together. I know you lied to her, Jaxx. Why did you tell her she was your mate when you cannot form a bond without your heart?" Cynthia asked, her body too close to me.

I needed to get away from this seducer. "Because she needed to hear it. When I had my heart, I knew she was my mate. And I do care for her deeply."

"But that is not love, and you should never tell someone you love them unless you mean it. You, of all people, know the consequences of telling false truths." She was right, again.

"What do you want from me?" Her hand moved to my cock. I snatched her wrist and growled, "Not that."

"So, you don't love her, but now that you have had her, you don't want another? As I recall, my skills are the best." She went to her knees and the memory of her sucking me came to the surface, but it was not her face I saw or her mouth but Abby's.

"No." My ears twitched with the sound of movement. I tried to step away but I stumbled and Cynthia climbed on top of me. I used my wings to knock her away, but she blocked it with a power I didn't know she had. Only Madam. "Stop it!"

"Jaxx?" I looked to find Abby standing with the blanket wrapped around her, her mouth agape in astonishment. Cynthia's eyes narrowed as an evil smirk spread across her face.

"This isn't what it looks like," I protested, finally getting to my feet. I closed the distance between us, but Abby held up a hand to stop me. Her eyes were full of pain that I never wanted to inflict.

"I can see now that I was a fool once more. Don't follow me." But I didn't listen to her. When I entered, Abby was nearly dressed and packing.

"It wasn't what it looked like."

"Fuck you," she snapped, shoving rations and clothes into her pack.

"Will you just listen to me? She attacked me."

"You're pathetic, Jaxx." I saw a slight tremble in her bottom lip. "Just leave me alone."

I snatched her by the neck, spinning her until her lips collided with mine. Something sharp stabbed me, and she tore her body from mine. Her dagger was sticking from my shoulder. Abby's tone was coated in hate. Her deep blue eyes alight with rage. "Never touch me again."

"Cynthia used her magic on me," I pleaded, dropping to my knees in front of her. "I'm telling the truth, Wildcat."

She looked away, then threw the sack over her shoulder, her brown hair cascading around her like waves. "I am done fighting for you, Jaxx. This was the last straw."

"But you must believe me. I am your mate."

"That's not what you told her." I followed her finger to where Cynthia stood watching the show.

"You heard us."

"Every single word. You manipulated me so that you would have sex with me. The funny thing is, Jaxx, I would have made love to you still if you would have just been honest from the start." She pushed past me to Cynthia, stopping, then punched her in the nose. Cynthia wailed, and blood poured into her palms. "Nobody follows me."

I leapt to my feet, packing my bags and pulling my hair back. "Where are you going?" Cynthia asked.

"To fix what you broke," I stated, unsure why I was still letting her speak.

"I needed to show her the truth—and you. Wouldn't I be dead if you had truly mated with her?" she asked. I didn't want to entertain her, but she had a point—not that I would ever admit it.

"Keep bugging me, and you just might be."

"Jaxx!" She stopped me in my path, and my wings flexed again as a warning. "If you want to fix what is broken, then you cannot go after her. You need to go on a different path."

"Why should I trust you?"

"I can show you."

"How?" I asked.

"I am a true sight, with many gifts, but let me show you. Allow me inside of your mind and you will see what must be done." I hesitated, and I knew about true sights although they were rare. None were in Dalaria anymore, as Rai saw to that massacre. "I will be gone, if you wish, once I show you your truth."

"Fine. Then I want you out of our lives for good. Also, you did not need to assault me to prove a point. Your punishment will come. Trust me, if not by my hand, by her, I can assure you."

"I've already seen my fate."

"Just get one with it."

"Let your walls down so I can come in." Cynthia touched my temples with her hands and I closed my eyes, slowly letting her in. The push of her magic was exhilarating, the flavor of ash filling my mouth as blurred visions flashed by. Expanding until they were clear. Past, seeing my mother and father again, reuniting with Calian, present, my time this past year with Abby, all the difficulties, making love that first time, and the future. My mate bears my mark. An obsidian crown with ruby embellishments sits on her head, and I, her king, wear a matching one.

Cynthia's voice echoed in my head, saying, "You must fix what you broke to achieve this future. Restore the bond or you will lose your mate forever."

I blinked several times after Cynthia stepped away.

"Do you know what to do now?" she asked.

"I do. But how do I get back?"

Cynthia held out her hand, and inside her palm was a single clear bean. "This is a portal bean. It was given to me by someone named Jack many years ago. Said he could not pay me with coin but adventure. I had a soft spot for him. Anyway, I've used one before and they work. You just need to imagine where you wish to go and it will bring you to it. But it only works once, so be certain."

"Why didn't you give this to us sooner? Abby and I could already be home," I stated angrily.

"Because she must retrieve the ashen crown. It is her destiny."

When she said that, the image of the crown my mate was wearing flashed through my mind once more. Even though I could not see Abby's face, it had to be her.

154

"She is the rightful ruler of Immorteum? How?"

"This realm was full of life before Rai did what he did. Not only did he tear Dalaria apart, but he came down here and cursed this land. We have been living like this for three centuries."

"What about the afterlife? Where does everyone go when they die?"

Cynthia shrugged. "I am unsure, but I know it is not here. The bogs are filled with the same reapers Rai placed in them. The souls are from the unfortunate beings that thought they could retrieve the ashen crown. Our last true ruler was King Alexxander Pendragon. This realm was called Dracane. He was a dragon shifter and his queen was a human. They ruled peacefully alongside his twin brother Arthur and Queen Gwenyfer of Constellina. But when Rai started the Dragon wars, he stole dragon power from anywhere he could get.

"Alexxander sacrificed himself for his queen so she and their children could flee. That is when they ran to Dalaria. Constellina was protected, as were the other realms of dragons and dragon shifters. I am not sure of what kind of magic, but more powerful than what Rai owned. Alexxander's child was the king who sat on the throne of Orion."

"Are you saying that Abbygale is the descendant of a dragon shifter king? She has dragon blood in her?" I asked.

"Your brother's mate is a goddess because he became a god when he died. They both had that blood within them; it needed to be awakened. In death, you are reborn. Your mate has dragon blood in her, and so do you. When she takes that crown and places it upon her head, the realm will be restored. Only if you are not there to combat the darkness, she will become a tyrant."

Cynthia's words had warning bells going off in my head.

"And that's why I need to restore my heart?" She nodded. "So be it."

I closed the bean in my hand, inviting Dalaria back to Orion to meet with Queen Kaleigh. The towers, the Orion horses, and the fresh forest snow. The bean fell to the floor, and a whirlwind of magic, lights, and air swirled around me. "Good luck, Jaxx, son of dragons."

Those were the last words she said to me as I jumped into the dark depths of the portal.

The impact of the stone ground knocked the breath from my lungs as my wings crunched. I slowly rolled to my feet, blinking to clear the fog. When I finally opened my eyes, an arrow was pointed directly between them, and two eyes so blue cut me like daggers. "Where is my sister?"

"Hello, Queen Kaleigh, we have a lot to discuss."

"Where is my sister?" she asked again, and I tucked my wings into me, making them disappear to get a full view of the room. Rowland was standing at his wife's side with his sword out, a full beard coating his face. Kaleigh looked the same except my eyes widened when I saw the roundness of her belly.

"You're with child?" I asked.

"You have fluff in your ears. Answer the queen's question—where is her sister?" Rowland asked.

"Your sister-in-law is more than capable of taking care of herself, as you well know, but she is in Immorteum," I stated, unable to look away from the belly. My ears twitched, and I tuned into the baby's hearts. It was strange to know that Kaleigh's was just slightly slower than her soon to be born twins. Yes, it had to be a girl and a boy with hearts beating at two different speeds.

"And you left her there? Alone?" Kaleigh asked. Then lowered her arrow to snap me out of my trance. "Great Kings, Jaxx, you act as if you've never seen a female pregnant."

"I have. I just try to avoid it when I can. You know that can be contagious, I hear." I then slapped myself for sounding like an idiot.

"Ah, I see a year in Immorteum did nothing for your intellect. Now, explain why you are here and she is there," Rowland said, putting away his sword away.

"Right. I think we're all going to want to sit down for this one. And drink. Oh, not you, of course." I sounded like a blabbering fool.

We entered the small foyer just outside the throne room. We all took seats around a table and I told them everything. Well, except the sex and other need to knows. I will keep that between Abby and I.

"And she must achieve this quest on her own?" Kaleigh asked.

"That is what the true sight said." I sipped on the grape wine, relishing the taste. Far more superior to the stuff Caine served.

"I see. Could you come here, Jaxx? I need to look at something."

I raised a brow, then shook my head. "No. Having one magical seer looking inside my head was an experience to last a lifetime."

"No need for that. I can see you are telling the truth, but you are keeping out details." The queen closed her eyes. A moment later, she opened them, only to glare at me. I chugged the rest of the wine. Was I afraid of Abbygale's older sister? Why am I acting like some virgin that got his wick wet?

"What have you seen?" Rowland asked, doting on his wife like always.

"He speaks the truth. My sister will return to us, but for now, we must help Jaxx get his heart back."

"We? You are about to give birth, are you not?" I asked.

"Have no fear, Jaxx. I will not be going, but Verglas will send a dragon with you. One of the smaller ones," she responded.

"Or Xiong," Rowland added.

"Fine. But the sooner, the better. I need to be ready for when she shows up."

Chapter Twenty

Abbygale

Fuck Jaxx.
Fuck Cynthia.
Fuck this realm and anyone who has ever betrayed me and my family. My heart was pounding as I pushed everything I felt for him deep down. If he wants to be a man-whore again, then that is his business, but I don't have the time or energy to give him any more of me.

I exhaled a deep breath as I marched on through Umbra Dolor. Avoiding all the sharpened boulders so I would not cut myself again. It was dark, but the torch I was using gave me enough light to see two feet in front of me. The scent of the bogs was drawing me closer, a mix of sulfur, rotting eggs, and death. Not that I could describe the smell of death any better than I just did.

The soul-keeper was safely secured in my pack. Giving up my soul to it just to retrieve a crown to have the power to fix the mistakes of the past and finally save the realm from Rai is something I just had not been prepared for. What is it going to feel like? Would there be a void? A feeling of emptiness? Or will it be like lifting this heavy burden from me? The mysterious nature of not having my humanity intact sounds more enticing than ever before.

The toe of my right boot knocked into a small rock

I did not see, sending me flying forward, but I caught myself rolling out of the way before being impaled on a boulder. Although I avoided instant death, my shoulder did not avoid getting cut by the pea-gravel that it scattered across the ground. A warm breeze brushed against my skin as I struggled to my feet. I reached over to feel the blood coming from the cuts of my exposed right shoulder.

"Fuck." My hand moved to my navel as I thought of Jaxx's fire sealing my most recent wound and I momentarily missed him. The warmth of his skin pressed against mine. His lips left trails of heat across my body, and the feel of him moving in and out, our souls connected on a deeper level.

"Stop!" I berate myself.

Quickly pulling my pack from me, I grab one of my daggers, pick up the torch I dropped mid-roll, and hold the metal part over the flame, heating it until it burned ombre. I took a deep breath and then pressed it to my skin. The smell caught me first, but I nearly blacked out from the pain. Jaxx could control the degree of his flames and there was little to no pain when he seared my skin closed.

A scream erupted from my throat, ripping through me as my flesh was burned. I blinked through the pain, as I heaved my breakfast onto the ground. Sweat dripped from everywhere and it seemed like I would pass out and never wake again. I tossed my dagger to the floor, picking up my canteen and gulping down some water before rinsing my mouth out.

I could really use some mint paste.

Once I gathered myself, I stood up again, my right shoulder protesting with every step. There was no set path to follow, but anyone who truly wanted to see the bogs never needed one. Very few people ever voluntarily came more because of the risk posed by the reapers. Little was known about them, just that if you got close enough for them to get their boney fingers inside of your soul, you are screwed. At that point, you might as well jump headfirst and become another lost soul of the realm.

I made it to the other side of the ridged barrier that separates Silva Corrupti Arbored, the city that is rumored to be full of the worse souls and creatures of the Immorteum. I glanced down the edge and noticed a single platform doc with a little wooden boat only big enough for two people. Making my way over, I noticed a faceless creature adorned in robes. Long, black tattered looking like they steal souls for a living.

"Excuse me?"

The creature turned its head to the sound of my voice.

"I assume you are to take me where I need to go."

No answer.

"I assume you understand me, but evidently you must be mute, so if you could use hand gestures, then that would be helpful."

No answer.

"Very well. I must do it all myself then." I reached around to my pack and pulled out the soul-keeper. Placing it at my feet and securing my pack once more, I lift it, flip it over and noticed some writing on the back.

It is in the tongue of the old religion, which I did not study.

"Great. Any chance you can translate?" I asked the creature and this time, it nodded. "Al right, now we're getting somewhere." I made my way to the edge of the boat, not getting in because of strangers, and flip the shield over for it to see. "All I need to know is how do I give my soul to this thing while it is protected, swim to the bottom of the bogs while figuring how not to die from lack of oxygen, and make it back up before anything happens to my body? Any suggestions?"

The creature spoke, sounding nothing like I expected it to.

"Abbygale Orion, princess, true-born descendent of the Great Dragon King Alexxander Penndragon, the ashen crown calls to you. If you wish to retire it, you must relinquish your soul to the keeper. Once inside, the only way to get it out is by the command of the one who loves you most. When you return with the crown, the realm will bow to your will. No one will resist your orders. Armies will rise in your name, countries will fall at your feet, and the realms of this universe will be reunited once again."

Well, okay then.

"So, I just need to go home and save it from a dark wizard. Being queen and all that is more suited for my sister, Kaleigh. I am sure you have heard of her. Great savior of Dalaria against Emperor Santanna." The creature let out an annoyed sound, and I stopped babbling. "Right. Okay soul-keeper, you want to protect mine while I go get this crown?"

It vibrated in my hands. The blue glow it emitted entranced me, but then prongs sprang out from the sides, pricking my palms with sudden, sharp pain, forcing me to drop it. But before it could clatter to the deck, the shield flew, punching me in the chest. My body flew backward, my back hitting the wood.

Stabbing pain like a hundred little pricks pierced the valley of my breast as it attached itself to me. There was a moment of darkness and, like an out-of-body experience, I watched as the soul-keeper cut my glowing soul from inside of me.

As I imagined before, it felt freeing. Like the weight of every burden I ever had was lifted from my shoulders and locked into this single box. The trauma of losing my first love, to fighting for my life in the Snow Forest, the wars, the battles, the betrayals, and broken pieces of my heart were all gone. I was the shell of my former self and it felt...amazing.

I am free.

My gaze lingered on the dark sky above me. Getting to my feet once more, I walked over to the boat and got inside. I knew exactly where to go because it felt like a beacon was calling to me. A ringing in my ears that only I could hear. The creature rowed, knowing where I wanted to go. It is crazy how magic works. I was grateful for the opportunity to use it. To learn from it.

We made it to the middle of the bogs, each ridged shoreline far enough away that the naked eye of a human couldn't witness what I was about to do. The bright green water illuminated with souls swimming about. Some crying in terror, others silent as they accepted the afterlife fate handed to them. I did not have to look at the creature to know what to do next. There were images of what would happen sent to me by the soul-keeper.

Everything felt right.

I held my breath before diving headfirst into the bogs. Every soul that swam past me, through, near me, felt like cold ribbons gliding against my skin. It did not remind me of swimming in a lake or ocean. The serene quiet that you get from letting your head fall under bath water was non-existent. It was loud and distracting. Screams and moans of pain are all I heard. My eyes did not burn from salt, similar to when opening them in the sea's water. But akin to when my head was above water. With every stroke I made, I felt the call of the ashen crown getting louder. It drowned out the noise from the others.

Then I saw it.

Black flames sat atop the crown of a skeleton with dragon wings. As I got closer, the tips of my fingers burned against the metal and a jolt of electricity shot through me. My grasp was within reach when something jerked my leg. I looked down to see a black faceless shadow with long boney fingers pulling me. I kicked at it, then it dug its nails deep into my flesh. An uncontrollable scream came from me and the panic of not being able to breathe seized me.

I kicked it away, and then I turned back to the crown. My legs begged for air. I kicked my legs, reaching out my left arm, but four more reapers came for me. Blood began to mix with the green of the bogs as it seeped from my wounds. When I finally got a hold of the crown, I fought my way to the surface. The darkness creeping in from the corners of my eyes was terrifyingly close.

This would not be how I died. I had the ashen crown in my grasp.

Then it clicked again.

I stopped fighting the reapers.

My body went limp except for my right hand.

Closing my eyes, I placed the crown atop my head and then let the magic take over.

I felt my body become paralyzed. Eyes sealed shut and magic vibrated all around me. The pain from the reapers disappeared. The erratic beating of my heart drowned the loud noise. This was it. There was no going back to the way I was before tasting this power. I finally opened my eyes and I was on the surface again.

I self-examined myself, noticing every wound I had was now a faint scar. I experienced a sensation of being healed all over. I looked at my reflection in the bogs, and there I saw it—the cool metal now gracing the top of my head. It was onyx black with a rhombus at the very center. The tips of each of its four points were sharpened, reminding me of the boulders in Umbra Dolor. But that was not the only thing that changed in my appearance. Streaks of red highlighted my hair and glittering sparkles of flames danced around my eyes, bringing more color to the deep blue.

I felt as different as I looked.

Stronger. Faster. Powerful.

My hands tingled with this feeling. I needed to unleash it.

The words came out annunciated; my ears heard them as my mind wrapped around each one, understanding the phrases.

"*Vara thal'kora en'ra thal'vyn.*" Ash filled my mouth as sparks came to life before my eyes. The wind picked up, swirling in front of me, as a mirage of fire and shadow formed a circle at the space in front of me.

Finally, it was time to go home.

Part Three: The Crown Of Ash And Shadow

Chapter Twenty-One

Jaxx

"And you're sure this will work?" Rowland asked as he looked down at the Dalaria map painted across the War Room table. They strategically placed soldier figures throughout the last known location of Rai's armies. They over took the northern territory of the realm, a large blockade cutting across Shuang, Zirian, Huo, and parts of the Snow Forest. Vergals had all the dragons protecting the border on our side once Rai sent his forces there over a year ago. Queen Kaleigh told me once Abby and I disappeared, Rai stopped all activity aside from taking over those territories.

"And you still don't know what's stopping him from going through?" I asked, while tracing the map. The craftsmanship was truly remarkable.

"No. One day, he and his forces just weren't able to go through," Rowland answered with a shrug.

"You ever think my brother and his wife had anything to do with it?" I asked, thinking of Calian...or Darius. Unsure of which name he is using now that he is the God of dragons. It was my birthright being the first-born son, but I would rather be down here living my life than having to handle the dragon race.

"It just seems that the day Abby and I disappeared, Rai got the dagger that can kill him, Calian and Emnera went to the temple of gods after failing to defeat him, to live their happy little afterlife while leaving us stuck to clean up their mess—a magical barrier seems to block him. I don't know about you, but from what I recall, those two would not leave us here without some way of helping," I added.

Rowland thinks on it, then nods. "I could consult my wife. Being that she has a strong connection to the gods and great kings than I."

"That is right. You have the gift of seers, too. What is the matter, once she got a hold of your co—"

"Be careful, son of dragons. You may have the powers of a dragon on your side, but I have the power of the realm on mine. One wrong move against me will be considered the highest form of treason." His intense glare told me he was serious.

I hold my hands up in surrender. "It was just a joke."

"We have no time for your antics," he snaps.

"Oh, but you clearly have time to fuck your wife enough to put a babe in her belly." *If he wants to play with fire, then he needs to prepare for the burn.*

Suddenly, the environment changed around us. The hairs on the back of my neck rose, my instincts telling me a threat is nearby. Wind blew hard around us but I cannot see where it was coming from. My hair whipped around me as my wings flexed on my back—then I saw it. A vortex of fire and shadow forming just in front of the door. A figure walked through and my eyes cannot believe what they saw.

Her eyes danced with blue and red flames, skin glistening with power, and an onyx crown sat atop her head. Those auburn locks now highlighted with streaks of red and black cascading in waves across her shoulders. My eyes trailed her body from head to toe and back up again, taking in the curve of her hips, the step of confidence with each stride. She looked radiant in the formfitting leather. But something was different. At the center of her chest, where my tongue had tasted many times before, was the soul-keeper. She wore it like a jewel.

The portal dissipated, and she walked straight to me. Without a single word spoken, her hand gripped my throat hard, and she brought my lips crashing against hers. She tasted of smoke and lust. My body came to life at her touch. I heard my inner dragon raising its head to find hers. But there was nothing there. Coldness replaced the once warmth I felt coming from deep inside of her.

When she released me, her eyes were alive with hunger and I momentarily was at a loss for words.

"What's the matter, Jaxx, don't recognize me?"

"Wildcat?" I asked. Only it was not her. Just the shell of the woman I once knew.

"Not anymore. Brother…" She waltz over to Rowland, unsure of who this person was impersonating Abbygale.

"Abbygale? Sister, is it really you?" he asked, astonished.

She smiled. "Not really." I watched as she made her way around the room without speaking. "I was once a woman called that. She was weak. Let her actions be ruled by her heart and soul. Now, I control those. Abbygale Orion is no more. You can refer to me as the Ash Queen because once I complete defeating Rai and his forces, only the dust from their bones will remain."

"You're here to help us?" I asked, unsure why I would question her loyalty.

She spun around. "Oh, Jaxx, you are intelligent sometimes. I am here to kill Rai, yes, but also to reclaim the realm. Since Dalaria did not aid my great-grandfather in the War of Dragons, bringing down the fall of Dracane, then this realm will not be considered my ally."

"Abby, what are talking about? This is not like you at all. Come talk to Kaleigh. She can tell you the truth," Rowland pleaded, but I knew from the moment I saw her that Abbygale Orion was gone. Taken over by some parasite.

"Abby?" Rowland has the powers to summon his wife because there she was standing in the forward. Her hand placed on her swollen belly. "Oh, little sister, you came home."

Kaleigh rushed to hug her, but I moved on instinct, blocking her. I narrowed my eyes at Kaleigh, hoping she would see the warning in them. "Step aside and allow me to embrace my sister."

"Yes, do as the Ice Queen commands," the Ash Queen said.

"Ice Queen? Abby, it is me. Do you not remember?" Kaleigh asked over my shoulder.

"You? How could I forget? Let's see." Abby tapped a long, black fingernail on her chin as she moved to the other side of the room. She wanted everyone's eyes on her and she got it. "How about the time you dragged me into the Snow Forest, causing me to be assaulted and raped and killed by a bandit? Oh, how about letting your best friend take my virginity without asking, so I guess I ended up getting raped after all, but I could not tell you because I did not want to ruin your friendship? Although, Tristan said I was far better than you ever were, so bonus points, I guess. Let's not forget about the war. The time seeing my first love get torn to shreds before my eyes. And you letting me get thrown into a realm with a dragon shifter I barely knew. Does that about sum it up?"

Kaleigh raised a hand to her mouth, her eyes brimming with tears. "Abby, I did not know about Tristian. You should've come to me."

I did not either. If he were alive today, I would kill him all over again—only he would suffer.

"She's lying," Rowland said.

I look between him and Abby. "Am I?"

Fuck. This thing was good at deception.

"You're not my sister. What have you done with her?" Kaleigh was angry now. I can see her power coming to life, tasted it on my tongue. But the Ash Queen was ready for her. Kaleigh soon gripped her head, beginning to fall, but Rowland caught her.

"You cannot enter my head, Ice Queen. I suggest if you wish for your children to come out of you alive, you leave me alone. I have things to go, people to kill, realms to take over. Dealing with my annoying past life is not on the list."

She left, but I would not let her go. Everything I thought I was going to have to do seemed impossible now. "Take me with you."

She raised a brow. "Why?"

"Because I commit myself to you." I started bending to my knee, a position I loved while tasting her on my tongue. "I, Jaxx, son of Tikka, devote my life to you, Abbygale Orion, for so long as I may live."

Magic zapped between us.

"Stand up." She gripped my chin, examining me, then smirked. "You will do wonderful things for me. Come, I have a wizard to kill."

I gave Kaleigh one last look that said I will save her sister. With her nod of acknowledgment, I knew I had her trust.

This time, I would not fail her.

The next time I saw Kaleigh Orion again, her sister would be at my side. Or I would die at her feet.

****

After walking through yet another portal, we landed at the inn on the blistering edge of the Snow Forest. On the other side were the deviated plains of Zirian. I felt the hum of magic vibrating from the barrier. I looked over at the Ash Queen as she ran her long fingers along it as though testing its strength.

"Seems like it keeps Rai in, but not his enemies. Come here." Everything in me wants me to defy her, but I do as I am told. "Give me your arm. I don't care which." I offered my left one, since I am right-handed. She gripped my wrist firmly, my skin coming alive at the sensation of her being close to me again. *I am so fucked*.

She used charcoal to draw a symbol on my skin. Rhombus, then she pulled a dagger. Her eyes met mine and I remain still as she cut the pattern into me. I'd do anything for her. My mind kept telling me it's not Abbygale. My mate is not inside of this body anymore, but other parts of me disagreed. When she finished, she repeated the same thing on her arm, then pressed our bleeding skin together.

"You know what a blood oath is, right?" she asked.

I nodded. "Good. Swear your life and allegiance to me, Jaxx. Be my Queen Consort, and I will give you everything you want and more."

Enticing offer.

"Give me my mate back, then you'll have me," I told her.

"Your mate is me. Everything you once cherished about Abbygale Orion is still here. I am just stronger and better than before. Trust me, you will have your mate when Rai is defeated."

"Swear it. Swear to me that after we have destroyed Rai and his armies, Abbygale Orion will be restored."

"So be it. You will have your princess."

"Then you will have my allegiance."

With that, the blood oath was sealed. I traced my fingers over the fresh scar and then watched in amazement as the queen worked her magic. Using words and phrases from the Old religion that I had never heard before, she cut out a slit for us to slip through. I tucked my wings in, following her.

On the other side was a vast army camp. Rai's enormous tower was just in the distance.

"What now, my Queen?" I asked.

"Follow. I will take care of the rest." And she did.

We walked in a direct path, her hands raised as she called flames and shadows—screams of pain, and the smell of death lingered in the air. A path of burned bodies, a pool of blood, and a destroyed camp were left in our wake. The power surrounding her was intoxicating, and I had never been more turned on than right now. Realizing my mate's magic was this strong. The ability to blend shadow and fire. She was going to kill Rai.

We stopped at the front door of the tower, and the queen leaned forward as if to listen. Then she turned to me, wrapping her body around me, and said, "Fly."

My wings listened before I could even register the command. I flew us to the only window at the top and we landed inside. Rai was waiting for us. In his hands, the chest that held my heart, and the dagger meant to kill him.

"I see you two made it out alive." He sneered.

"Shut up, Rai." With the wave of her hand, Rai was knocked to the wall, the dagger and chest falling to the floor. I went for the chest and dagger, but she stopped me as well. "No, no. You stay over there."

My back hit a wall, and chains wrapped around my wrist and neck. The iron burned my skin. "What is this!"

"It's keeping you from being a hero," she answered.

"I get to kill him! You swore it."

She chuckled. "No, I said you'd have your princess back, and you will."

The Ash Queen walked over to where the dagger was, picked it up, and approached Rai. "Look at you, the great and powerful Rai brought down by a mortal. How does it feel knowing you are going to die soon?"

"I will come back. Just as I have in the past," Rai said.

"Tsk. Tsk. Not this time." I watched as the Ash Queen whispered another incantation to the dagger, and it shone a bright crimson.

"That is not possible. Only the Ash Queen can wield it on me," Rai stammered. Seeing him tremble in fear made me happy. But this was supposed to be my revenge kill, not hers.

"No more talking."

I fought against my chains as she placed the dagger right over Rai's heart and slowly plunged it in. I watched as the light in his eyes disappeared. Then his body burst into flames, a pile of ash at the queen's feet.

She spun around, dagger in hand, while picking up the chest, then came over to me. "So, this is where your precious heart is."

The queen stopped by my left hand, placed the edge of the dagger against it, and sliced my palm.

"Fuck you!"

"Quiet!" she shouted. My blood dripped against the chest and then it opened, the steady heart beat emanating. I felt my blood flowing through me, calling out to the main chamber that kept me alive. Everything was heightened as her fingers delicately held it in front of me. "This is going to hurt you, more than it will hurt me."

She shoved the organ through my chest. I screamed as the pain took over me. The chains rattled as I trembled. Every vein latched onto the organ and all my memories of the past year with Abbygale hit me like a blast of fire. The feelings I could not always express or understand every time I looked at her. When her skin pressed against mine as we made love for the first time. And the way she looked into my eyes, so deep in love.

I finally caught my breath, and when I opened my eyes again, I saw her. "Wildcat?"

Chapter Twenty-Two

Abbygale

"Not exactly," I responded.

If only Jaxx knew how hard it was to fight the power inside of me. I was cruel to my sister, I know that. And the lies I told about Tristan tasted like acid on my tongue, but the moment I saw she was with child, I knew I had to push her away or else she would have followed me.

"What have you done with her?" Jaxx growled.

"I think I enjoy seeing you in chains," I teased, and I did. Seeing him like that was stirring all sorts of feelings in me.

"What is going on? Why did you take my revenge kill from me?" I could see the hurt in his eyes and I wasn't sure if I should feel guilty or not.

"You were not the only one he hurt, Jaxx. Now I have defeated him. We can move on with our lives." I reached for his chains, unlocking them. He nearly fell to the floor with weakness, but recovered soon enough.

Before I could move, my back was against the wall, his dragon claw wrapped tightly around my neck, his large wings flexed out as he snarled at me. "You have three seconds to tell me where my princess is, or I'll rip her out of you."

"Kill me, and the princess dies too." I was battling

with the soul-keeper's magic. The ashen crown adding to the taste of dark magic. But I needed Jaxx to believe a part of me was still here.

I reached up a hand and traced the stubble along his jawline, down his chin, then over his lips. "It is me, Dragonboy. I am right here."

His eyes widened slightly before his lips collided with mine. There was nothing sweet about it. Our tongues clashed and his hands slid to my hips, lifting me with effortless strength. I wrapped my legs around him, my fingers tangling in his hair. I went for his shirt, discarding it first, then my fingers roamed across the corded muscles of his chest as his mouth moved to my neck. I tilted my head to the side, granting him access to mark me.

He pulled my zipper down, leaving me bare, and soon after, he joined me. My back pressed against the wall as he positioned himself perfectly at my entrance, and plunged deep in one single movement. "You are queen now, but I am the master of our fucking bed. Got it?"

"Yes," I moaned as I held on to him. My skin came alive with each thrust, every touch. I felt him in me, on me, and something was trying to break free from my chest. That is when I realized the soul-keeper was still attached to me. Something was blocking us from connecting fully, and it was my fault.

"Oh, Wildcat, I have wanted to claim you for so long. Now you can bear my mark alongside yours." His whispered words were coated with desperation, but all I felt for him was pure, unrestrained lust. I needed the release, so I remained quiet. He thrust faster until his seed exploded inside of me.

He pulled out of me, then placed his forehead against mine. This was supposed to mean more, but without my soul...

"What's wrong?" Jaxx asked, looking at me. Then his eyes drifted to where the soul-keeper was and recollection hit him. "You didn't feel a damn thing for me, did you?"

Should I lie?

"No, Jaxx. This was all about lust," I answered honestly.

Hurt coated his features, but then he kneeled at my feet, taking my left ankle in his hand, and tossing it over his shoulder. My toes barely touched his inner wing. "That means you did not come. And that is unacceptable."

Before I could protest, his mouth was on me. His tongue licked me from clit to entrance, diving in and out. I gripped his hair, needing to hold on to something as his finger found my clit. Rubbing and licking. Sucking and bringing me close to the edge of bliss. "Ride my tongue, Wildcat."

And I did.

Shamelessly, I moved my hips back and forth, the feeling intensifying as he inserted two fingers, pumping them in and out. His three plunged in to my ass, making me feel full. When his teeth nipped my clit, I came undone. My thighs tightened around his head. When I finally came down from my high, I turned away from him and picked up my clothes.

"How do I fix this?" His words were whispered against my skin. His naked body pressed against mine as I fumbled with my clothing.

"Fix what?" I asked.

"You are my mate, Abbygale Orion. Mine. Not some magical artifact." I turned around to face him and before I could protest, he was pinning me to the wall again, his mouth claiming me once more. "Mine. These lips." He moved down to my breast, sucking each one. "These breasts." Lower. "This body." Again kissing my pussy, then back up to meet my gaze. "Mine."

I swallowed, then stood as tall as I could. "This crown and shield are mine and I belong to them, not you. I am sorry, Jaxx, but as the Ash Queen, there is nothing you can do to overpower me."

"I am not giving up on you. What about this?" He raised his arm where our blood oath was made. "You wrote to give her back to me."

"And I did. You got your princess back the moment you plunged your cock into this body. You shouldn't have been so vague about your meaning. You, of all people, should realize the magic has grey areas. Little loopholes."

"No. No. No. I will not accept this."

"Too late, Jaxx. If you want to have any life with her, then I suggest you come with me," I stated, after getting dressed again.

"Where? Rai is defeated. There are no enemies."

"There is still one false queen I have left to deal with back in Immorteum." He raised a brow, and then shook his head in disappointment and realization. "She must die, as well as that little whore who dared to betray me."

"Cynthia? She helped us."

"Is that what her mouth all over you is called? Helping you to come?" I asked. Jealousy was a human feeling; I should be feeling nothing. The princess was fighting back.

"Believe me or don't, ever since I made love to Abbygale the first time, there has been no one else I wanted," Jaxx admitted.

"Just get dressed. We need to leave soon." I walked away from him to go to the window, my back to him as I looked over the horizon. The barrier was still up, which meant I had Rai's armies to deal with. A thought crossed my mind at that moment. I could use them to face Lady Sotto and take back Immorteum.

"Change of plans, Dragonboy. We are staying."

"What about Lady Sotto?"

"She can come to me. Fetch me all the generals in Rai's armies. It is time for the Ashen Queen to show everyone who is the rightful ruler of all realms."

****

Jaxx did as told, and in an hour, five generals were lined up in front of me. I examined them from my throne, which I added a cushion to because how could Rai sit on something so hard?

Each one was a unique creature: an orc, shadow beast, dark elf, human, and Minotaur. "What are we doing here?" The orc snarled, his tusks long enough to poke his black eyes out.

"Because I ordered it," I answered.

"And you are nothing but the human queen's little sister. You have no power here," the orc general argued.

I released an annoyed sigh. "Bring him to me."

Jaxx forced the general to his feet, then dragged him to me. "You don't know who I am, but you and everyone else will soon figure it out." I stood, looking between all of them. "You will all serve me and my conquest. I intended to destroy anyone in my path. I've invited the false queen of Immorteum to our world. Once she arrives with her armies, we will go to war."

"And what of the Ice Queen? Will you do what Rai could not?" the orc general asked.

"My sister is not a threat."

"We will only serve the one that will help us take our realm back. Dalaria has never belonged to your family or the others that have claimed it," he said, and the other four shouted in unison.

"You are fools to think that this realm was created with you all in mind. No, it belongs to the dragons and therefore, it belongs to them. I am mated with the son of Tika, which means I am a dragon ruler. Not only that, but my crown would not bond with me if I did not have dragon blood running through my veins. So let's focus on the task at hand. Everyone will wear my brand. If you refuse, then you die.

"If you think there is none to replace you, well, you would be wrong again. You are wondering if you are so powerful, why not do it all yourself? Well, I intend to. For now, you will ensure all your troops know who I am. When I call you to war, you will come without question."

They did not say anything, just gave each other looks, and I knew I had to make an example of what my power meant. I snapped my fingers and the orc general burned to ash right before their eyes.

"My queen."

"Long live the queen."

The chorus of praises resounded in my ears, and I knew I had it locked down.

****

My skin was alive again as I moved my body up and down, sinking deeper into Jaxx's cock. This is what he wanted, a connection with his mate, even though I can feel nothing but lust for him.

The black silk sheets of the enormous bed were a subtle change to the ones Rai had. There would be no way I was sleeping where that evil bastard slept.

Jaxx's fingers dug into my hips as he bucked up, then his mouth clamped down on my right breast, sucking and teasing. A moan escaped me loud enough to echo throughout the room. "More, Jaxx."

In a split second, he flipped us, plunging into me, and I relished every movement, in and out. My heels dug into his butt, one of his hands rubbed my clit faster, matching the pace of our movements. I needed more. Something gripped a hold of me on the inside. A warm light was coming to the surface, and I could not fight it. Abbygale's soul was reaching out.

Jaxx bit down on my neck hard enough to draw blood, and I blinked. Then she was there, piloting our body. I could see her. "Jaxx, more pain. I need more."

"More, Princess?"

Instead of words, she moved for him to stop, then flipped over, reaching around to grip his cock and press it to her ass. We were not prepped, but that was the point, wasn't it? "Now."

Jaxx didn't hesitate, plunging inside of us. My control was faltering. "Fuck."

"Jaxx, more." He slowed, and I gained control again. "No. You must hurt me. Spank me. Hit me. Bite me."

"What? No, I am not hurting you." He stopped completely.

"Please, don't stop." She was crying now. "The pain. It…" Abbygale's words trailed off as I snuffed her light out, taking back control. "Continue."

"What?" He pulled out, and I flipped over, then straddled him, lining my ass up to his cock and sinking down. He groaned and I captured his lips before he could ask any more questions.

I moved his hand to play with my clit, plunging two fingers in and out as I rode his cock, bringing us both to climax. My body shuddered against his as he spilled his seed in me. We flopped to the bed, catching our breath, but I did not stay long. I headedto the large bathing tub, dipping inside to clean up.

Jaxx approached and got in on the other side.

"Is there something you need to tell me?" he asked.

"No, Jaxx. Nothing at all."

Chapter Twenty-Three

Jaxx

Something was different about the Ash Queen.

Wanting me to hurt her then acting is if it were okay. It had been a week of nothing but fucking and waiting. Not that I'm complaining about getting to taste my mate any chance I get.

I missed the witty banter between Abbygale and me. She was this stiff queen with corrupted artifacts, draining the goodness out of her. At this moment, we were quietly eating breakfast while she read reports from the generals as we waited for Lady Sotto and her armies. Part of me did not want any of this to disrupt our bubble of routines, but I knew it was not truly real. My arm was branded with a symbol that did not resemble our mate bond. Which did not feel completed at all because I did not have the real Abbygale with me anymore.

There had to be a way to rid those artifacts. A theory to test would be the pain one. What if it were my mate's soul trying to reach to me? Can I hurt her body just to save her soul?

"Jaxx, the longer you stare, the less appealing your company becomes. If there is something you would like to say, open your mouth and speak."

"Why did you ask me to hurt you yesterday?" It

came out straight forward because I don't beat around the bush.

She dropped the paper, folded her hands in front of her over the placemat, and smirked. "Oh, Jaxx." She stood, sauntering over to me. Her hand ran along my shoulders. "I thought we'd try something new." Her lips caressed my ear before she whispered, "But f you're not the adventurous type, then perhaps I should find someone else."

I was quick to dispute that.

I leapt from my seat, gripped her neck and forced her onto the tabletop, giving a rat's ass about all the dishes falling to the floor. Her legs opened to me as I took a single claw of my free hand and pulled her pants off her body. I pinned her arms to the small of her back, then ran my hand over her plump ass. "You see, I don't fully believe you."

My claw punctured her skin, and she squealed out. I then lifted her up so her back was pressed against me. My free clawed hand skimmed over the skin of her navel, digging just enough to draw blood. There was a shift in her eyes. So I dug harder, and she screamed in pain. "Jaxx! Jaxx!"

"Wildcat?" I asked.

"Please, you have to rip it from my chest."

"What do you mean?" My grip lightened.

"More pain, Jaxx. It is the only thing subduing her." She was shaking in my grip and I hated seeing her tears shed, knowing I was causing it. "More pain or I'll lose control."

I let my claws go deep enough to where she would heal, but I caught nothing vital and winced at her screams. "Tell me what to do."

"Take…it…out." Her breathing had grown ragged. I felt her pulse pounding in my hand, and the smell of her blood nearly sent me into a killing mode. "The shield."

I looked at it before withdrawing my hand from her neck, digging my claws beneath her skin to grasp the shield. I hesitated for a second then kissed her deeply. "Don't die on me, Princess."

"Do it."

I ripped the soul-keeper from her, blood and skin coming with it. It fell to the floor and shattered on impact. Quickly, I placed my hand over her open wound and let my flames heal her.

"Abby! Abby!" I shook her, attempting to wake her, but her eyes remained closed. "No! No! No! You will not leave me. I will not lose you." I placed her level on the table, my ear to her chest to find a pulse, but there was nothing. "You must live. I cannot lose you." Her cheeks were wet from something dripping, and I looked up, expecting to see rain. My face felt hot and damp—It was me. I was crying. I leaned down to kiss her, trying to give her the breath of life, but she remained still. "Please, you cannot leave me. I…I love you. I need you. You are my mate, Princess. Mine."

Gentle hands gripped my cheeks, forcing me to lift my head, and I was met with a smile and two dark blue eyes taking me in. "I've waited so long for you to tell me that with your heart beating in your chest."

My lips collided with hers at that moment. Our clothes discarded on the floor soon after and I carried her to the bed, gently laying her down. There was no more time to waste. Our bond needed to be solidified. I knew it and so did she. I continued kissing her. Our tongues danced as our bodies joined in passion and heat. Her skin pressed against mine and I knew it was real between us. She writhed beneath me as I plunged in and out of her, claiming my mate truly.

"Say it, Princess. You must claim me as I claim you. Only then will we be truly mated," I whispered against her skin, leaving kisses all over.

We slowed briefly as she looked into my eyes, full of love and admiration as she whispered her vows into the universe. "Jaxx, you're my mate, now and forevermore." She moaned into my mouth as I kissed her, my mind cluttered with visions of our future.

"Abbygale Orion, you're my mate, now and forevermore." I sped up as her heels dug into me, her hands gripping my shoulders, pulling me closer. We came together, magic coming to life as our symbol imprinted over our hearts.

A moment later, her head lay on my chest as her fingers traced over the tattoo. "I thought it would be the Orion and dragons or something. Why is it a green rhombus?"

"Well, the ashen crown claimed you, and so did I. The green stands for me and my flames, and the rhombus is your new symbol as the ash queen."

"But I don't want to be a queen."

That was a relief. I truly had my mate back.

"You're my queen, whether you want the title or night." I moved to look at her. "And I'll worship you all day, every day, just as you deserve."

She smiled this time. "Easy, Dragonboy. There's still a war coming to the realm. We need to be prepared."

"We are, remember?"

"The armies, yes, well, probably should not be fighting an evil army with another evil army. I don't think it will work out." She had a point. "Besides, now that we're officially saved, we should just runaway, find a small place and live as commoners."

"You don't mean that," Isaid, while moving a strand of hair from her face.

"Yes, I do." Her eyes reflected seriousness.

"But you would miss the birth of your nephew and niece. And I have a feeling you don't want to miss your chance at being an aunt," I reminded her.

Abby nodded but went silent as she played with the curls of hair on my chest. "After all this war business is over, we are leaving to find a place of peace. I wish to build a life with you. A meadow to grow flowers, a forest to hunt game, and a small log cabin to fill with love and warmth. I will visit my sister, niece and nephew every so often, but my future is with you. Not sitting on some throne."

I smiled and my ears focused on one minor detail. "Don't bite my head off for asking but, when you mean to fill our home with love, did you mean children?"

Abby sighed, then pushed to sit up. "I'm unsure if I wish to bring children into a war filled with danger."

That was valid.

She stood, grabbed the silk black robe from the wardrobe, and wrapped it around herself before pouring a chalice of wine and turning to face me. "If I don't want to have children, will it make you love me any less than you do right now?"

"Nothing you could ever do could make me love you less. You don't wish to have children, fine. I get to keep you all to myself." I moved to join her, not wearing a robe because I fully planned on taking advantage of being naked with her as long as I could. "But if you were to ever change your mind, then I'll be here to do my duty as a husband and a father."

"Husband?"

I walked over to where my wardrobe was separate from hers and grabbed the box. "I was waiting until the right moment to do this." I took her hand in mine then opened to reveal the custom emerald rhombus ring I had made for her.

"When did you have the time?"

"Well, we were in Immorteum for a year, and every day, I walked past the jeweler. That ring stood out to me, and something inside told me to buy it. There was only one person I ever wanted to give it to, and that was you." I knelt on the floor and looked up at her. "Abbygale Orion, Princess of Orion Fortress, Ash Queen, will you do me the honor of becoming my wife?"

"Yes!" Abby leapt into my arms, kissing me all over, and then I pulled her to me, placing the ring on her right middle finger—customary for our culture. "It's absolutely beautiful."

"Just like you."

****

Two more days passed before we got reports of Lady Sotto and her army arriving far north of Zirian. Abby and I had stayed occupied, celebrating our engagement naked, and because of the Ash Queen's threats, no one disturbed us.

"I'm going to have to keep pretending to be the evil Ash Queen, right?" she asked, weirdness laced into her tone. We were waiting in the throne room for Lady

Sotto to grace us with her presence. Abby had been pacing for most of the hour, and even my hair was standing on end.

"Calm down, Wildcat."

"What? How can you be at ease right now? I can't pretend to be evil." She gave me a look of disbelief. "I can't do this. I was fooled to go after the crown. We both nearly died. I would have handled our bond never forming, and the future of Dalaria would be lost. I can—"

I pulled her to me, shutting her rambling with my tongue down her throat. "You talk too much, Wildcat."

"Jaxx—"

"Shh. You need to relax." I moved to kneel before her. She was dressed in a warrior outfit fit for the queen. Long skirts not too heavy, with knee-high boots laced up. I bunched up her skirts, then pushed her legs open to reveal herself to me. I pulled her lace cover aside, then dipped my tongue between her folds, licking her pussy.

"Jaxx, there is no time. Oh, gods." She moaned, her hips moving.

"Ride my tongue, Wildcat. You feel so much better afterwards." Her hands tangled in my hair as I licked her up and down, my teeth teasing that little bundle of nerves. I added two fingers to her pussy, pumping in and out as her hips picked up the movement.

"Jaxx…" I loved hearing my name come out in a raspy tone. *I am going to make sure she knows just how much I enjoy the taste of her.* My ears twitched as the sounds of multiple footfalls came from the tower stairs. I couldn't help but smile. "I'm so close." I bent my fingers, finding that spot she loves, just before the doors opened. She came onto my tongue. Her hands gripped my hair tightly.

I was quick to move her skirts back but stayed on my knees. Lady Sotto would need to be afraid of my mate. And I was going to make sure of it.

"What's this?" Lady Sotto demanded, as she saw me acting like a whipped dog at the Ash Queen's feet.

"Don't be jealous, Lady Sotto. My pets don't just obey me—they worship me." I licked my lips on queue and I saw Lady Sotto trying to connect the dots.

"I see. I did not expect you to have the power of a dragon god. But I can see I was wrong," Lady Sotto said. sounding surprisingly humble.

"Oh, don't fret. I am going to offer you the chance of a lifetime." Abbygale assessed the room. "Everyone leave, except for the Lady and my pet."

None of Lady Sotto's men obeyed, but then Abbygale narrowed her eyes. "Dismissed."

When only the three of us remained, I stood. Going to my mate's side, she took my hand in hers, kissing it. "What is going on?"

Abbygale turned to look at the woman, who was shaking in her heels. My mate stood and approached her, not stopping until there was nothing but a foot of distance between them. "You are going to make a peace deal with my sister, Queen Kaleigh. Dalaria will not see war any longer than it has."

"Why would I do that?"

"Because you want to be Queen of Immorteum, do you not?" she asked.

Don't give your crown to her, Wildcat.

"Yes. But the ashen crown chose you."

"And I will choose my successor. Dalaria will

know you. You and I will restore Immorteum to the realm it once was: Dracane Kingdom. I will not dishonor my family's legacy by continuing to keep it cursed. Agree to peace and I will give you power to see over Dracane. Do we have a deal?"

Lady Sotto did not move, but her eyes kept going between the two of us. "He isn't your slave, is he?"

Abby smirked, then raised her hand to reveal her ring. "No, Lady Sotto, he is my mate."

"You have dragon's blood and are mated to the son and brother of the god of dragons. I have no claim to the Dracane Kingdom once it's restored."

"Are you refusing my offer?"

"Yes. I am afraid to say that I am." Lady Sotto sighed. "I know you don't know all our history but, only a dragon can claim a throne that belonged to a dragon. The land will remain cursed unless a dragon takes the throne back."

Fuck.

"Fine. You will join my council. First, we need to eradicate the beast unless they sign the peace treaty as well. I need all my generals to come to Orion Fortress. We will all sign the treaty with blood. No one can break a deal sealed in blood. Unless they wish to die."

Chapter Twenty-Four

Abbygale

Lady Sotto stared long and hard at me. I could tell by the persistent flicker of her eyes that she was weighing her options. Follow me or die. That was all she had to choose from, and it would be the same choice for my generals.

"Very well. Call upon your sister. Tell her peace is coming to Dalaria."

I offered my hand to her with a smile.

She left the room, and I turned to Jaxx, a sly smile painting his charming face. "You were fit to be queen."

"I still don't want it," I admitted.

"Well, queen or not, command me to be on my knees and I'll obey it every time." Cheeks heated and my core throbbed at the memory of how his tongue felt against me just a short while ago.

"What if the generals don't agree?" I asked.

Jaxx sauntered toward me in that animalistic way he has always moved, then gripped my chin, lifting to meet his eyes. "If you wish for me to kill them, then I'll present their hearts to you as a gift. If you wish for me to burn them, then my flames will light up the sky in your honor. Everything that I do from the moment our bond was sealed will be for you. I meant it when you asked me what it meant to be my mate."

I smiled as the memory came to life. "Remind me."

He returned my smile, his wings flexing around our lips, a breath of a whisper away from touching. "Death to anyone who harms you. And you belong to me as I belong to you."

Our lips collided with a heat of passion.

"I will never be done loving you, Wildcat. Never get tired of tasting you on my tongue, feeling you clench down around my cock as I leave my teeth marks on your breasts." His hands moved to them, pinching my nipples. Then he lifted me into his arms. "And if your womb ever fills with a child, then I'll be the luckiest man alive all over again."

We made love in the throne room, but managed to reach the bed chambers before falling asleep. It was the middle of the night when I sent a messenger bird to my sister, knowing the barrier would not stop it—just as they have always been able to fly through such wards, as was once the case with the barrier that divided Orion and Zoldir. My long nightgown fell to the floor and the stone beneath my feet felt cool.

I went to look at the looking glass in the bathing chamber and peeked at Jaxx before placing a hand on my belly. The signs have been present since the first time we made love. There was no protection being used as we were caught up in the moment and at first, I was afraid of the truth of it. And I think when I went into the bogs, there was a moment of what if I was wrong? Would this hurt it? Would I be happy?

Mother always told us when we were girls that a woman always knows when the time comes. Our monthly blood stops first, then there's the sickness, and other heightened senses. Wanted to chalk it all up to stress and magic possession, but my new power had given me the ability to do what I thought was impossible.

I closed my eyes, placed my hand over my belly just above my pelvis, and listened. There, just faint enough to hear was the rapid flutter of two hearts beating inside of my womb. When I opened my eyes, I realized I was crying again.

"Wildcat? What's wrong?"

I turned away from him, wiping the evidence of my emotions. "Nothing." It was too late.

He wrapped me in his arms. Then he saw the streaks. "Who has upset you? Shall I kill them? Give me a name."

Wow. "You'd be killing mc then."

"Never. Why have you made yourself cry?"

When I looked into his emerald eyes, I wondered if our twins would have them. Would they be boys with the same dark curls as his? If we had girls, would they look like me?

I looked down at our toes, trying to suppress my tears again, and I knew if I did not tell him, he would find out soon.

"Jaxx," I started, and it came out choked. "I…I…"

"Shh. Come here." He was so warm against me. I was safe in his arms. I knew that. This would not break us, but what if war came? He would never let me fight, not that he could stop me. But would I risk the death of our unborn children just to prove a point? "You don't need to tell me. Tell me when you are ready. When the time comes, I am here, whatever it is."

****

"We will not yield to a human queen," the dark elf

general exclaimed.

"Neither will the rest of the armies. We will fight for our right to live in these lands just as before," the new orc general added.

"You act as if this is your birthright. Santana and Rai created all of you out of magic. I'm unsure why you all didn't perish with them, but you didn't and now you must be dealt with. If you don't bend the knee and agree to peace, then all of you will die on my orders," I stated.

"We will fight you to the death," the dark elf general snarled.

"So be it." I narrowed my eyes, then without them realizing fully who they were dealing with, my daggers went flying. The first two connected with the orc and dark elf generals square between their eyes. Jaxx had already set aflame the other three. Lady Sotto was trembling where she stood, but she had nothing to fear from me. "The rest of their armies will die."

I made my way down the steps to meet the five regiments with one-thousand soldiers each. Even the humans would perish because they were not humans no more, but corrupted by dark magic as I was. I climbed onto the raised platform to address them with magic that would allow all of them to hear my voice.

"Soldiers, I am your queen. You will bend the knee before me or perish. Make your choice." Some looked confused, but others understood right away and fell to the ground. "All who remain standing will die in three...two....one."

My power connected with about one hundred from each regiment, and as I used the magic the ashen crown gave me, I could feel the moment their bones shattered, the blood evaporated from the heat of my essence, and all that reminded in their spots was a pile of ash.

"The armies have been purged. My sister has returned with the signed treaty. We cannot disturb her as she has begun the throes of labor," I told Jaxx. "We are finally at peace."

"Shall we head to Immorteum?"

I shook my head. "It is time for me to claim my birthright. Dracane Kingdom will be restored."

With Lady Sotto and our armies in tow, we all moved through the portal I summoned with ease. There was nothing but silence once more, as I remembered it when I last left nearly two weeks ago. But Lady Sotto had taken everyone with her aside from Cynthia. Which I needed to deal with at once.

After getting settled into the palace, the armies dispersed throughout. I followed Lady Sotto to the throne hall. I had to perform the ritual that would break the curse. Jaxx was by my side as I waited, staring at the onyx throne that matched the crown atop my head. "Queen Abbygale Orion, you must place your hand on the symbol. Recite the vow of the dragon, and then the curse shall be broken."

I nodded, then released a heavy breath.

"Allow me," Jaxx said. He took my palm, then gently extended a dragon claw and made a cut, offering me a wink that promised fun for later. He then stepped back. I did as Lady Sotto said, then grabbed the parchment and read aloud.

"I, Abbygale Orion, descendant of the dragon king, Alexxander Pendragon, do solemnly swear to rule the Dracane Kingdom with mercy and truth, justice, and love. Keeping up with the laws and traditions set forth by my ancestors."

A wave of magic vibrated from where my hand was on the throne, crashing into everything and everyone. It was as if my body was standing in place, but my soul floated, watching as the kingdom changed. The harsh ridges of Umbra Dolor changed into a beautiful meadow of flowers. The forest where Jaxx and I came together finally changed into a blooming area filled with various fruit trees. The transformation of the bogs from a reaper field lake to a crystal-clear view also occurred.

Every harsh ridge or surface changed into something beautiful. The palace was transformed into a striking volcanic stone, with a lava fall visible in the distance. Even the commoners' quarters had transformed into a better city for them to live. When I returned to my body, I blinked away the lingering fog and then caught the sight of my two blazing emerald eyes taking me in.

"My queen." Everyone fell to their knees at my feet and Jaxx came to me.

"Well, they can never question your birthright now. Look." He pointed behind me and just over my shoulder, protruding from my back, were beautiful black dragon wings with crimson colored bone tips at the ends.

"What? How? Why do I have wings?"

Jaxx leaned down and took me into his arms. "There is so much to tell you, Wildcat. And I cannot wait to show you just how much fun having wings truly is."

"To answer your question, Your Grace, you are a Dracane Queen now. Which means your dragon blood has become more dominant inside of you, giving you the appearance of a dragon at any time," Lady Sotto informed me.

"You know a lot about the history of this realm, don't you?"

"Yes, Your Grace, and it would be my honor to teach you," she said with her eyes averted.

"Yes. I think it would be wise for me to know more about this place. Cannot rule if I don't know the people. It would not be right." Jaxx winked at me. "Everyone is dismissed. If anyone needs me, I will be in my chambers. But don't disturb me unless it is an emergency."

Without protest, Jaxx and I headed toward our chambers. A large room with a four-poster bed and crimson silk sheets. It was simple, and I liked it. A bathing chamber and a wardrobe for each of us. Jaxx crushed his lips to mine as soon as the door was bolted shut. My fingers wentto his clothes as he undressed me. I felt my wings flexing, but I had no control over them.

"What's going on with them? Why won't they stop?" I asked.

Jaxx smirked, reached out with his wing, and barely touched mine. A burst of ecstasy came over me and I moaned loudly. "I told you that our wings are extremely sensitive."

"I believe you now." I pushed him down on the bed, crawling over him, then licked him from his neck down, relishing in the salty taste of his skin. My pussy was throbbing, but I needed to taste him.

"Turn around." I did, and we positioned ourselves so that his mouth claimed my pussy. His fingers danced along my wing and I nearly came all over him. I sucked his cock to the back of my throat, then toyed with the edge of his wing. He bucked into my mouth, causing me to gag. We went on like that until I came on his tongue and he exploded into my mouth.

We fell to the bed. Jaxx pulled me into his arms but my wings were still out, but he avoided them. His hand fell to my belly, and I sighed, then I got up. "I must tell you something. I should have said it sooner but with all the impending doom, I was not sure if I could." Jaxx came to the edge of the bed then pulled me into him placing a kiss on my lower belly on the right, then on the left. His eyes met mine, and I realized he already knew. "How long have you known?"

"I heard their hearts beat after the night you came back to me."

"Why didn't you say anything?"

"Because I knew you would when you felt you were ready."

"Is that why you asked me to marry you?" *Please don't let that be the reason.*

"Fuck no, Wildcat. You are my mate and I asked you to be my wife because I am so fucking head over heels in love with you."

My heart jumped at that affirmation. "Twins, Jaxx. We're going to have twins."

"I know."

I kissed his lips hard this time, moving to straddle him. He was ready for me, so I sank down onto him, needing to be close once more.

"I love you, Wildcat.

"I love you, Dragonboy."

A word about the author...

C. M. Hano is a Fantasy Romance Author who aspires to write strong female-driven, hot, and magical adventures and be a good mother. She lives in Louisiana with her husband and three beautiful children.